Spectral Visions: The

Edited by

Colin Younger

with

a Foreword
by
William Hughes

ACKNOWLEDGEMENTS

The Editor would like to thank the contributors to this volume both for the excellence of their contributions and for the patience they have displayed while this book has come to fruition. I am also grateful to colleagues at The University of Sunderland for their support of Spectral Visions, notably Professor Ian Neal (Associate Dean of Faculty), Dr Alison Younger and Dr Susan Mandala of English Studies and Anne Lambton (Team Leader of Combined Subjects). I am also indebted to colleagues outwith Sunderland who have supported Spectral Visions from its inception, amongst them Professor William Hughes, Professor Willy Maley and Professor John Strachan. My most notable debt is to Steve Watts (Head of Department of Culture) who has tirelessly supported our work and has been pivotal in the development of Gothic Studies at The University of Sunderland and David K Newton a constant friend and supporter of Spectral Visions. Finally thanks go to our students, 'The Visionaries', without whom Spectral Visions and this attendant volume would not have been possible.

SPECTRAL VISIONS: THE COLLECTION

CONTENTS

Foreword - William Hughes	iv
Weaving the Wyrd - Alison Younger	1
Blood Moon - Willy Maley	8
The Curse of the Creator - Mary Ross	11
Kiss of the Vampire - Steve Willis	17
Crimson Blade – MikeAdamson	18
Memento Morti - Colin Younger	37
Green - Kirstie Groom	44
Where is she? - Paul Alderson	45
A dream in a Cemetery - Franklin Charles Bishop	51
Returning - John Strachan	61
The Promised Bride - Janet Cooper	62
The Victim - Glenn Upsall	67
Welcome to the Hell Hole - Lindsay Bingham	70
The Ghost of Strawberry Hill – David Craig	79
The Damned – Katie McMahon	82
Temptation - Nicola Rooks	83
Laura - Michelle McCabe	86
White - Kirstie Groom	88
The Inn - Jamie Spears	93
Last Call - Elizabeth Hazlett	103
Shadowraith - Steve Willis	105
Dance of Death - Josh Christian	111
GH3 - Caitlin Wilson	116
Smile - Chloe Charlton	121
Us - Caitlin Wilson	127
The Magdalene Asylum - Conor O'Donovan	129
The Journeyman - Lee Mitchell	134
Notes on contributors	137

FOREWORD

WILLIAM HUGHES

The anthology or collection of shorter tales is one of the great traditions of the Gothic. Though it is true to say that the Gothic began in 1764 in the form of a novel – admittedly the comparatively short novel that is *The Castle of Otranto* – it was not a long time before that work, in the form of derivative, adapted, or heavily edited versions, became a component of larger blue-book collections. These works, typified by relatively short fictions, with sometimes two, three of four narratives punctuated by intense action and high emotion included within a total extent of less than sixty pages, arguably made the excitements of Gothic available to the wider reading public and set the genre at the centre of a profitable trade with regard to both the booksellers and the circulating libraries of the eighteenth century.

The nineteenth century witnessed the eclipse of the blue book and the rise of the ghost story as the basis of any respectable collection of supernatural narratives, the Victorian ghost story itself being customarily of a longer length than its eighteenth-century equivalent. The customary culture of such collections changed somewhat at this time also: ghost story collections became primarily an exhibiting space for the short work of a single author – J. S. Le Fanu is probably the supreme example of a writer remembered in this way in the twenty-first century – though the tradition of the association of supernatural works by several hands survived quite satisfactorily under the aegis of monthly journals such as *Blackwood's*, *All the Year Round* and *The Strand*.

The twentieth century regenerated the anthology first through the advent of thematically focused serial publications such as *Weird Tales* and later through the rise of cheap paperback collections which variously revived interest in the short fiction of earlier authors or else introduced readers to those writers engaged in extending the reach – and the topical focus – of the traditional tale of terror. Such volumes as were published from the 1960s by imprints as diverse as Pan, Sphere and Fontana, under the editorship of writers such as Robert Aickman, Herbert Van Thal and Richard Dalby, are still read and collected today, and are in many respects as significant to the current revival of Gothic in popular culture as their blue-book predecessors were in its initial dissemination. Though many of these collections style themselves as anthologies of ghost stories, it should be noted that most offer a mixed economy of spectral tales, the horrors of human depravity and the revival of folk-tales and mythology. In many respects, they are more closely related to the products of the eighteenth century than they are to those of the nineteenth.

Spectral Visions: The Collection sits squarely—and honourably—within the great tradition of Gothic anthologising. Like its earliest ancestors, it is the product of creative minds well versed in the stylistics of a form which, while relatively consistent, is never static. Like many of the later collections that perpetuated the heritage of the eighteenth and nineteenth centuries, its components are provided by diverse writers who, variously, already enjoy established reputations or who are currently engaged in the active and vital process of crafting those reputations. For some of these authors, fiction is an adjunct to writing in academic or other spheres; for others, it is the basis of a remunerative career or else germane to a personal identity that sets them aside from some other, probably more onerous, occupation. For all, participation in this volume is a lively and positive contribution to the vitality of a genre that is approaching 250 years of demonstrable popularity—a popularity which has resisted the dismissals occasionally levelled against it by elite culture and moral self-righteousness alike. Long may this resistance continue. I commend *Spectral Visions: The Collection* to you as a starting point, if not for your own creative intervention into Gothic stylistics, then as a catalyst to the development of further critical appreciation.

William Hughes
Professor of Gothic Studies,
Bath Spa University.

WEAVING THE WYRD.

ALISON YOUNGER

> Hail he sang, hail he who understands.
> May he use them well who has grasped them,
> Hail those who have listened.[1]

It's cold. The hunger has gone. I no longer thirst, and my body, now naked is without sensation other than the piercing cold which gnaws at my mutilated fingers—no nails—and mangled feet. I see the livid wounds from the boots and the nubs of bone reaching through the blackened flesh. I don't feel it. All I can feel is the cold, and all I can think is that it will, it must end soon. "Element of Fire I call you here…"

The ceasing to feel came late. When my eyes grew accustomed to the darkness I realised I was among others, slumped against the walls, weeping and jibbering in the molten blackness, filled with the scratching and rustling of minute feet on putrid straw. "Sister" she said, "you are not alone", and I reached out into the livid night, I felt the broken hands—once young, and understood. A hard black pellet of wax and hair is pressed into my bloodied palm. "Take this" she said, "for when your time comes".

My time is come:

> You stand accused of the making of diverse clay pictures, the one for the destruction of the young Lady Buchan, and for getting her enchanted, and for the shooting of elf-arrow heads at diverse and sundry persons. For making a stoupfull of poisoned aill for the performance of your devilish malice, the which when it fell to the grasse which grows made it to dye immediately… Confess!

"They will say" she said "that you are in league with the devil… that you have the strength of the evil eye that carries a curse in a greeting". Somewhere in the blackness that has seeped into my mind I remember: the charm, the *eolas*, the cure, learned at my Mother's knee, and she at hers:

> Be the eye of God betwixt me and each eye
> The purpose of God betwixt me and each purpose,
> The hand of God betwixt me and each hand,

---

[1] Havamal.

The shield of God betwixt me and each shield,
The desire of God betwixt me and each desire,
The bridle of God betwixt me and each bridle,
And no mouth can curse me.

The eye of the envious will split the stone. Turn the curse. Return it. Remember. The charm of the thread: *Eolas-an-t-snathlain*. Spin and chant. Twine the wool, red, blue and green. Speak the benediction. Give to the afflicted. Turn the curse.

I fear the hex. It brought me here. I know the ways of cure and protection. I know how to guild and grace and charm. "Do good only" said my Mother, for the devil has set the dark ones in his kingdom to cast sickness and death on man and a blight on the beasts. Fear it." We sang to the stars and saluted the morning sun and the new moon with joyous welcome. In the circle of stones we joined our voices, wanting justice:

> Thou shalt arise early and go forth afield. Thou shall take thee to a boundary stream that shrinks not in heat, in parching sun, in drought of summer. And though shalt dip thy face in the stream three times in succession. And after that thou shalt bathe thy countenance in the nine gentle rays of the sun. Thou shalt say thy prayer and proceed to the moot, and no matter, no might, between ground and sky; between heaven and earth, shalt prevail against thee, shalt have effect on thee, shalt oppose thee, shalt keep thee from what is thine.

The 'one who kept apart' caused the withering of fruit and the drying up of milk in cattle and women. The others whispered "*Air-an-chronachadh*": these are 'the harmed' by the eye of the ill-wisher. Grim and forbidding she arrived like a harbinger of evil in the Wolf month, followed by purple clouds, dank and evil which emptied themselves on the village, distorting the trees and summoning the storm-demon to raise the winds and break their backs. Brooding and bloodless she swept in on the storm; her fleshless and featureless face appearing nothing more than shades of leprous white and unfathomable dark. The tempest followed her to the moor where she set up a shelter, which grew, by no human hand to be a dwelling, and on each moon one of her sisters, two swart spinsters arrived, creeping, drifting like a malevolent mist on the moorlands. The elders barred their doors, for they knew that the devil and his consorts danced and drew down the moon on the moor, and the Nine Maidens, turned-to-stone, flinched and skulked away from that unhallowed place. And the cursing, stronger than any of our charms could counter, clutched the heart of the landscape with its deathly hand until the newly-born beauty of the coming spring was sMothered in its cradle and all was lifeless and fallow.

They are with me now, those dark sisters, pale as the grave and perched liked ravens in the shadows crawling forward only to hiss blasphemies and abuse the thing in the hood. The curse, when it comes drifts into the livid blackness, first a whisper then a roar as each of this corrupt coven joins her voice to her sister's in macabre recital: "*Ghabh an droch shuile e*"—the evil eye take him. The words float and fall like poisonous vapours in the foetid air, reaching their ghastly fingers towards the thing in the hood—once a man—who readies his instruments, impassive, cold, and unaware of the coiling, seething hatred that touches him tentatively before engulfing him absolutely. I have no love for my abuser, but I know their ways and I fear their evil, so as the silent chanting becomes deafening I whisper the cure:

> The eye that went over
> And came back,
> That reached the bone,
> And reached the marrow
> I will lift from off thee…

I cannot complete the blessing as he stops my mouth with his filth-encrusted fist. The other, equally rancid is entwined in the matted wool that used to be my hair. "Curse away witch", he snarls as I'm dragged, not protesting over the rough flags. Momentary relief as the hands, benumbed by days in what they call the strappado are released. For the first time in days and nights (how many I cannot say) I sit. Cold wood, slicked with warm liquid absorbs me into its being and my hands are pinioned with hemp.

My soul is being cleansed. I am purified by pain. All that I am is pain, a living hissing pain which coils around me, grasping me with burning pincers, scoring my face 'above the breath', ramming itself deep into my flesh; into my most private places and ravaging the raw wounds where my fingernails used to be. I cease to be human as the *cashielaws* lacerate flesh and crush bone with each insistent thud of the thing in the hood. I smell blood, taste it as it catches in my throat, slaking my thirst with gore as my body twitches in a grotesque parody of dancing on immobilized, marrow less legs that will dance no more. Trapped in the bowels of the earth I focus on the words: "Element of Earth I call you here…"

Before I died in this place we danced in the ring to the music of the piper in the pastures among the hills. Thrice tossing the reaping hooks in the air the gatherers drove the cattle through the Beltane fires so that they could be cleansed of all evil. We, the girls carried *gris-gris,*[2] filled with Dragon's blood and Dulce seeds to draw a lover, and we braided the rowan with threads to aid the raven to build her nest and the lark to sing. The elder women, wove the web of the wyrd, twining the threads in their teeth while crooning runes to chase herring into the nets of the men. At the waxing and waning of the moon we danced with the dryads of the Oak, the Elder the Willow and the Rowan whispering their secret names: '*Dur, Ruis, Suie, Luis*' in a litany of life without end. But here, in this chair made of cold, dead wood the spirits have taken flight, and my life is ended. As Death creeps closer I welcome Him as an old friend come to lull me to sleep and end the pain that I have become.

"You are not dead, Sister, your time is not yet come" she hisses, teasing the powder, softened with spit between the shreds of my lips. I sense, rather than taste comfrey, kidney-vetch, screaming mandrake and dog violet absorbing her humming incantation to knit the dissevered pieces of flesh that I am. In the magic circle of light trickling

---

[2] A small bag made to carry the wishes of the carrier. Dragon's Blood is a concoction made for the same purpose.

from the wretched stump of a candle she feeds me from the withered, nodulous lump of her third teat; her flesh inscribed with the sigils of torture around the devil's mark. The eyes, enormous and dark in the blasted wreck of her face stare back at me, like the wild eyes of the *Cailleach-uisge*,[3] wrathful under the waterfall, as deep and shadowy as the loch. She is a cunning woman—a wild hag with a venomous aspect who beats at the crops with a stick of sorrel who disappears in a cloud of angry passion if she is caught in the first rays of the sun. Daring ourselves, we sought her wands in the whin bushes, and we hunted her in the scrying pools where the *Caesg*[4]; sinuous, silver-scaled, half woman, half grilse swim. She is here now, naked like the Caesg, unclothed like me lest some fiend's poppets have been stitched into our clothing. But we unlike them have no hair which has been shorn for fear it conceal the devil's brand, licked, they say onto our scalps and secret places to suckle the imps of the Deceiver. As I'm anointed with tears and blood; my own or hers, I cannot tell, I open my third eye to my second sight.

I'm sinking in the scrying pool. Tied cross-wise, thumbs and toes, my ravished and desecrated body is dragged down, down through its obsidian surface in dark tides to the home of the healing naiads, distant, divine but ever closer. In the pale violet subaqueous light of these Stygian waters they come to baptise me into human death. Twice more have I reached this sacred place, and, as my lungs learn to breathe the liquid air I am borne, purified and placid towards the soft silt of my resting place. As my vital spirit leaves me in one long exhalation the waters scorn me, spasming and gasping into the arms of the men with the staffs and the ropes. I am cast out of Heaven and thrown to legions of screaming demons assuming the figures of the loutish crowd baying 'burn the witch'; for the King's book[5] says:

> ...that God hath appointed ... that the water shall refuse to receive them in her bosome, that have shaken off them the sacred Water of Baptisme, and wilfully refused the benefite thereof.

The wind becomes a roaring traveller, dragging the dark clouds; now helmets of darkness, across the blushing face of the sun, and the waters churn like a cauldron of vapours as the men in black pronounce my fate... I am lighter than water. Element of Water, I call you here...

She has confessed, and for this they will stop her breath before consigning her to the flames. At her grandmother's bidding she renounced Christ and had congress with the Devil; half man, half satyr, shouting blasphemies and twitching in rapturous convulsions in an icy union which left her gravid with evil. Enthroning Him as her Lord she had danced widdershins and incanted from a diabolical grimoire to call a demonic horde: Satanas, Beelzebub, Lucifer, Elimi, Leviathon and Astaroth: spewed from a

---

[3] A vindictive water woman.
[4] Freshwater mermaids.
[5] James 1 of England. Daemonologie (1597)

Hell-mouth to parade and cavort in devilish and blasphemous procession to the Kirk. With her hellish sisters, she had rifled the tabernacle, and stolen the ciborium in which the Sacrament was reserved and mixed it with the seed of man and the courses of woman in an unnatural and maleficent Eucharist which gave them the power to fly and to sell fair winds to the sailors. She had venerated the Fiend and made blasphemous and abominable conjurations. She had bled unbaptized babies, snatched from the cradle, rended their flesh defiled their bodies, and roasted the carcasses to harvest the tallow to savour her food and nourish her unholy offspring who cavort by night as cats and owls. They slaughtered travellers, sacrificed to their perverted tastes. When the old Laird desired the young Lady Buchan she had butchered a wolf and taken his private members and the hairs from his body and boiled them with the brain of a murdered infant in the skull of a suicide. The monstrous concoction, having fermented for three days, she gave to the Laird who gave it to the Lady so that she should desire no other man. Her soul, snatched cruelly from the arms of Christ was taken, shrieking by the *Sluagh* to join their unhallowed and diabolical procession.

The Sluagh[6] are assembling again, their rotten souls an abomination so foul that even Hell cannot stomach them. They drift shadow-like, winged demons on the westerly wind flinging lightening and glutinous rain; fathomless avian shadows with skeletal fingers and serpentine hair who suck the souls of the unshriven dead. They will gorge this day on these three unhallowed and raving sisters who are being carried, naked, polluted and denuded to the cleansing flames. An aura of filth and death engulfs them as they are carted, gibbering and cackling in turn to their place of execution.

The mob is restless as the abominable trinity hurl profanities at the solemn minister who calls for repentance and casts down his eyes to avoid their maniacal and baleful stares. The pyre waits: sulphur-infused faggots of straw and wood awaiting the touch of the executioner. They are dragged from their hurdles, one-by-blasphemous-one and the battle for their corrupted souls begins. The King of the elements is pouring his wrath upon the earth as the rope is drawn to stop their breath. Purple faced, thrawn and desiccated they are tied to the stake, while the Sluagh, sensing food circle overhead, and swoop in the plumes of miasma that seep from the rain soaked faggots surrounding the unholy dais. The sky, slashed with red wounds joins hands with the reaching flames in a fatal union as the three are roasted in the infernal conflagration. Then a cry, hideous and grating, belches from the parched lips of the third—not quite dead, frying in her own unholy grease. The winds, in league with the too-green faggots turn the flames from her to prolong her suffering and she mutters as she melts, even when her tongue is swollen and her lips are shrunk to the gums in her blackened, boiling face encircled by a perverted halo of red beams. As her bonds burn she claws at her breast with the broiled excrescences that used to be fingers until the cooked bones can hold the weight

---

[6] Souls of the unforgiven dead

no longer, and the arm, shrunken and seared falls into the living flames, made strong by the fat, water and blood which drip from the ends of her remaining fingers. The skin of the nether parts is stretched and opened and the bowels, sizzling and stinking fall out while still she mutters and the covetous Sluagh hiss impatiently for their prize. Muscle and meat are replaced by white bones as the flesh falls away in gouts of red and black, quickening the ravenous flames, meat-fed, carnivorous and seething around the charred stumps that had once been legs. The mob gag and salivate as they swallow the liverish stench of burning meat—the incense of abomination, as she is sacrificed, still twitching to the ravenous *Sluagh*.

> I know the third; if my need grows dire
> For binding my deadly enemies, I dull the blades
> Of my foes—neither weapon nor deception will bite
> For them,[7]

My people are rune casters—seers, spae-wives and Sybils who read the sacred Ogham and weave, in words webs of protection. Hagalaz is the rune of protection and shape shifting. It protected us, for a time from their spells and curses. The charm was broken when my Father, clan leader was found murdered; butchered and emasculated on their monstrous altar, all gore and corruption. The lips, in the chalk white face were drawn back in a snarling rictus which gave the appearance of a feral sneer and from between those dead lips the aroma of loss, tainted with Monkshood, the Devil's Helmet[8] floated like a threat in the dank air. The unkempt grey pelt of his hair was twisted in tendrils around the nails which had been driven in to the hilt. His hands, clawed in agony are nailed in like fashion to the four poles of the flat rock to which he is pinned, unmanned, unmade and no more. The *caoineadh*[9] of the woman echoes and rebounds around that dark place in a choral lament of divine madness and my Mother, soul-bound, barefoot and dishevelled, throws back her head and her eyes gleaming with a wild and savage look howls a *coronach*[10] to mark his passing. Hers would follow—self-murder by Aconite within a cycle of the moon. Leaderless the clan scattered to the four poles of the forest leaving only me and the three sisters to face the dark-clad vengeful men who tied us, tortured us and brought us to the rank, dank confines of this place of death.

---

[7] From Hamaval.
[8] Wolfsbane.
[9] Weeping, lamenting
[10] lament

It is cold. I stand at the axis at the circle's centre, callow, pale and soft-bodied, awaiting my final ecdysis. I am tired of this bloodied and broken form and I yearn to be rid of it. As the fire is lit I call upon the guardians: Earth, Air, Water and Fire and they come, gnomes, sylphs, undines and salamanders, dancing in the scented air: Basil, bay, bergamot, Bouganvillea, and broom. Notus, the kindly wind carries my song to the Great White Goddess; Andraste, Anu, keeper of the silver wheel of stars. The Sluagh cower from her opalescent light and flee, freighted by the foetid souls of the dead-departed clutched in their rancid talons.

Soon. Soon. Andraste's iridescence is consuming me, drawing me into a moon-struck union of body and spirit, radiant as the flaming Djinns assist my transformation. Bathed in Her silver light I entreat Brid the Goddess of Fire to work her alchemical magic in the forge of my being.

Soon. Soon. Emboldened by the Djinn's craft the salamanders strip me of my mortal form like the attendant maids of a bride on her wedding night. Veils and swathes of skin and sinew fall around me while the wind hails my passing by casting the scents of carnations, hibiscus, nasturtiums, and poppies into the silvered air. My human exuviae is being sloughed away, food to Lycaon, as my shattered bones knit, strengthen and lengthen embraced by muscle and sinew. There is a stirring in the empty and ravaged nail beds which stretch to accommodate the claws which force the last vestiges of useless skin from the leathering pads of my hands. Long silver hairs, mimicking and reflecting Anu's healing rays caress my body, wolf-kissed, lupine, about to be born.

Soon. Soon. The veil of my body's temple is rent as I feel the shining canines pressing through my virgin gums and I step, transformed from the flames into the panicking and awe stricken mob. Newly born and lethal I turn my wolf-eyes on my tormentors who cower under my gaze, and the last sound they hear is my birth-cry, an ululation of sheer exhilaration which resonates and carries on the four winds to the waiting ears of my scattered pack awaiting the gleeful savagery of wanderer's calling.

BLOOD MOON

WILLY MALEY

I'd been feeling ill. No, not ill exactly, just tired and hurt, heart-sore hurt, like dental pain in the chest cavity. Not sleeping hasn't helped. We see eye to eye on so much, but her worship accusation had blinded me with anger. And she was confused about why I kept asking to see the writing about her dead lover, if it left me hurting. I didn't want to be a sponge, a soak. And since I'm used to being without, doing without, going without, I decided to take a step back. I hid, but she found me out with her evil eye and her pointy fingers. So I took a deep breath, read all her writing again and with each word felt those fingers squeezing my heart, wringing it dry. I threw the scalding pages into a drawer and headed out. The sky had changed. It seemed the moon was shining rather than the sun. Even the birds sensed it.

    I met my brother and he asked what was wrong. I realised I was walking hunched over, like I had a body on my back, like I was carrying a coffin. I was distracted, half listening to him, thinking about her, when she sent a message asking if I was thinking about her. That witch was trying telepathy on me now; playing with my head like it was a football, the woman that didn't like sport, the world's greatest sportswoman, Sportswoman of the Year. I went back to work, took a class, distracted, distraught, drawing on years of putting on a brave face. Lines in texts flew out at me, slapped me around the head, made me wince:

> Nor Mars his sword, nor war's quick fire shall burn
> The living record of your memory.

Then just when I thought it couldn't get any worse she sent me another of her tales tall and true. Her unsporting behaviour included kicking a man when he's down. But I had to read. I had to.

    When I finished I went straight to the toilet. I looked in the mirror. There was a welt on my neck like a rope burn. I'd been struggling to breathe as I read, and it felt like someone else's fingers had been round my neck. I stumbled home in the dark and went to bed, knowing I wouldn't sleep, might never sleep again. She had performed her sorcerer's art with the photographs, the clothes, the songs, the stories, the puzzle box of tricks she had given me, just big enough to hold a beating organ, like a heart. I got up out of bed, crawled to the door, went down the stairs to the street. Going over the bridge, I took the stupid smart phone from my breast pocket and threw it in the river. "That's it gone forever", I shouted. It had brought me nothing but trouble, made me a zombie living in a bubble. I felt sick and threw up and the wind carried vomit out and up into the trees. I wiped my mouth and carried on. When I reached the dark tower the wings of the gargoyles appeared red in the glow of the traffic lights below, and as I glanced up it seemed the moon itself was caught in the same bloody glare.

Back in my study, I started with the puzzle box. Never mind pussyfooting. I broke it under my heel, heard it crack and splinter, then tore up the contents, the ones I could tear up, but the way I felt I could have ripped through brickwork. Same with the CD, deleted the songs, the poems, shredded up the writing, stuck it in a bag, together with the piece of black silk, the death cap. To think I thought it was another garment. Then came the hardest part, I took a pair of tweezers and stuck them in my right ear, right up to the fingertips. I bit my left hand to stop from screaming, took off two fingers in the process. I had to push it in so far I was holding onto the end with my fingertips, but then I heard the click of metal on metal as I pulled something out. It was the size of a five pence piece but it wasn't a coin. It was a small silver disc with strange scratches on both sides, like hieroglyphics. I put it in a ring and spun it, and sure enough there it was. "They can put pennies on my eyes when I'm dead", I said out loud, but nobody's going to find this. With a pair of pliers I cut it into eight pieces, one for every lying letter. Then I took the bag in my stumpy hand and kept the slivers of metal in my right fist. I walked down the hill in the direction of the café. It would be closed, of course, but no matter. I'd never darken its doorstep again. It was on the blacklist of places never to go back to except at pistol-point and even then I might take the bullet rather than go in. But I needed the walk. The streets were empty. I put bits and pieces in every bin I passed, including one piece of the disc. When I put the last one in I felt something come up into my throat and tasted metal and salt. I panicked and stuck my hand back into the bin. Something bit me – a rat or a squirrel, a rodent of some kind, no doubt something she'd conjured up with her cards and her candles. I pulled my finger back out and started sucking the blood, the iron tang of it bittersweet. I looked at my fingertip under the streetlamp, covered in little scratches, like the disc.

I took my glasses off, held them in the three remaining fingers of my left hand so I could focus. Something started to spin, but I couldn't tell if it was the finger or my head. Surely a finger can't twist like that, even if you're dreaming, even if you're dead, not if it's still attached to the hand. Different if it was off altogether. Then I realised it was one of the fingers I'd bitten off. It had been in the bag. I was twirling it in my good hand. It spun, spelling out my fate. Then it was true. There was no escape.

I walked back up the hill, retrieving all the stuff from the bins as I went. The rats and squirrels knew better than to trouble me now. I'd follow them to their nests and squeeze them all to pulp with my seven swollen fingers. It had taken me five minutes to shred the stuff. It took me five hours to put it all back together. The disc went in last. At least I had tried. I did one last thing before I slipped it back into the wet grey pocket behind my right eye. When they dig that small circle of silver out of my head at the end they'll find scratched in tiny letters with a needle the one word: Help.

Ironic, because they'll know that nobody heard till it was too late.

THE CURSE OF THE CREATOR

BY MARY ROSS

You will triumph over everything done against you. Ptah has overcome your enemies. They no longer exist.
Chapter 166 the Egyptian Book of the Dead

Western Thebes: in the time of the Horus kings.

In the fading heat of Ra the wailing of the hired mourners stifled her. Nanu leant on her sister Nitocris as the *sem* priest, clad in the leopard skin vestment of his office for the dead, completed the rites for her daughter. Her tears pleaded with the creator Ptah that Shadya would pass safely through the fearsome Gates of the Tuat, and that she would be judged worthy at the Tribunal of Osiris in the Hall of Ma'at, so her *khu* eternal spirit could shine forever, one with Osiris himself. She begged Anubis to keep Shadya's *khat* body in the tomb safe, so she could live with the gods forever. In a short time, she thought, she would join her daughter and beloved husband Amasis, True of Voice, in Aaru, eternal happiness. She shuddered. She herself would have to pass the dread Gates, cross the Lake of Fire, brave the terrible demons that haunted the way and then avoid the forever death, in the jaws of the demon Ammut. Fainting with the thought, she leant on Nitocris to have strength to leave the remote wadi. To linger would risk them both becoming prey for the evil spirits she knew prowled the falling night.

Aaru (the fields of heaven)

I, Thoth, scribe of Ma'at, the upholder of the balance of truth and justice, and companion of the gods, record the admission of Shadya, True of Voice, to the eternal loveliness prepared by the gods for those who survive the stern test of Ma'at which no liar or thief can cheat. In the forever now, Ra shines without scorching; the sweet northerly breeze cools their faces and abodes; fields of rich fertility feed them without any effort; they hunt, race, and sail on the face of Mother Nile without risk of harm. Their beloved pets are always with them, playing in the sun and shade, and the wild beasts, placated at last, are their companions. In the evenings, they come to their homes of millions of years to find food and wine prepared and rest waiting. Drought, famine, war, want, sickness, pain and death have been swallowed by Ammut the Dread Destroyer at the command of Ptah, the Creator of All. All their loved ones are with them in harmony and joy.

The True of Voice give thanks at every moment for the bliss of being. They have forgotten their pain and are one with the gods. In the heavenly village, their earthly lives seem like a dream, not remembered.

And now, Atef, the *sem* priest who was the friend of Nanu's family in life, is with them all in Aaru as he shares their tomb in love on earth.

Thebes, three millennia later...

I Thoth, record what I see to bear witness at the Tribunal.

Men can again read the sacred writing, and know of the gods and Ma'at.

Surely they will uphold Ma'at. The curse of Ptah falls upon any who do not.

March 1900, Cairo.

At last I have achieved what I came for—and more; five mummies—two adult males, two adult females and a young girl, perhaps a family from the paintings on the cases. They will share my cabin on the journey from Port Said to Brindisi and on. Soon I, George Robinson, will be a wealthy man!

Evading Maspero's Antiquities Service was infernally easy. I was worried the sealed mummiform coffins would be too large to smuggle out of the country safely, but as a prize the find was too great to ignore.

The fellahin who found the mummies were stupid peasants, easily tricked with threats of being reported. Heaven knows I need the money more than they do. These mummies will be the making of me! I will arrange public unwrapping ceremonies. My quack medium will tell the newspapers that she has spoken with the dead ancients to boost ticket sales—and then there'll be the sale of the amulets from the bodies, the ornate coffins and the bodies themselves—still valuable ground-up—for medicine if a better offer is not forthcoming from a private collector. Who knows—I might make a habit of it if there's enough money and fun in it.

Soon I will replace the money I was cheated out of at the gambling table and have the cash, clothes, gifts, and the ability to cut a dash to convince my sweet innocent orphaned Heiress Susanna and her deaf elderly aunt to bestow her family's fortune on me.

Soon I'll be a wealthy bridegroom!

But first, to finance the public unwrapping. The young woman is the least impressive of the five for a public event, but she'll be bound to have amulets, her mummy-case is nice enough, and it will be easy to sell the body on. I'll grind it up myself if need be. As soon as I am on the steamer at Port Said…

Aaru

In their home in Aaru, all is not well. Unease gives way to malaise. Nitocris and Nanu cannot say why, but weep – something never before witnessed in heaven. Ameris has nothing to say. The worst is Shadya: disoriented, listless unable to think.

Atef worries but says nothing. Their tomb in Thebes has been plundered. Worse, much worse could happen—and they are powerless to prevent it.

Horror-strengthened, Atef dresses himself in his leopard skin funeral robe and casts himself into a trance:

> I command you, my *ba* spirit, take your bird form and descend into the tomb. There find my *khat*. Find out who has violated our rest!

The *ba* descends but finds no *khat*, only a mean, wood-carved head, thrown aside by the tomb robbers. The tomb is empty.

His cry to Osiris is heard; Osiris himself feels the tear in his being as the family's eternal existence is threatened.

Tuat (the underworld)

I, Thoth, descend from Aaru, to Tuat, to the judgment hall of Ma'at, commanded by Osiris.

In Aaru the family of Amasis are under attack from living men. Time has intruded on eternity.

Amasis, Shadya, Nitocris, Nanu and Atef shine less brightly and they once again feel worry and pain. Their *khat's* have been removed from their graves. Their eternal souls—their very existence—are in jeopardy and they know it. Ptah himself, their creator, is insulted with the threat of their extinction in all worlds.

Anubis, messenger of the gods, must once more return to the land of the living.

Aaru

Waking from his trance Atef at once sees that Shadya is worse. She is cold, and clutches at her breast, unable to stand. Nitocris and Nanu lay her on a cushion. Atef divines that an evildoer is removing the protection of her heart scarab. Should he remove the djed pillar talisman—the guarantee of her stability in Osiris—she might lose all consciousness, and then it would be too late:

Quickly, Shadya, you must command your *ba* to find your *khat* wherever it is while you have strength. See who is doing this. Speak to his mind, show him your immortal beauty and beg him to return your protection. Warn him he will be punished, but if he stops he may yet be saved.

The Peninsular and Oriental steamer "Osiris" en route to Brindisi

Shadya finds her *khat* on board a ship by the blessing of Osiris whose name it bore. At once she speaks to George Robinson, *ka* to *ka*. George hears her appeal, though his *ka* is coarsened and sluggish with vice. It cuts through the drinking and gambling session he is enjoying with the occupant of the adjacent cabin and some other young men, right to his own heart:

I beg you by the gods of the Two Lands; return my amulets that we may both live.

George downs his whisky and calls for more—refusing to accept that the words are anything more than an over active imagination requiring more alcohol to subdue it. But the voice in his soul refuses to be quietened:

Please, by the great Osiris himself – return my amulets before it is too late.

George staggers to his feet. To his companions' consternation he cries:
It is too late – I have lost it in this game of cards – reclaim it not from me, I beg you, but from its new owner! Here – here is Robert Johnson!

... and with that, he flees to his own cabin.
    Shadya's *ba* has no strength to return to Aaru. She must enter her ruined *khat*. If she can speak with him then she can seek strength to return to Aaru. Desperate she reanimated herself and seeks to plead with him. But George had violated her mouth with rough hands seeking treasure and the words will not come. She struggles to sit up, clutching her throat. If she could only...
    George crashes his oil lamp into her fragile body and springs back as flames leap fed by the very resins her Mother had lavished upon her for her safety. Shadya's voice returns now in the agony of fire and fear. She shrieks to Osiris and Ptah for justice as she is annihilated in all worlds, forever.
    George beats out the flames and throws the remains into the sea before taking breath. Turning back, he sees a jackal-headed figure in the shadows before his consciousness flees from what he has done.

The Judgment of George Robinson in the Hall of Ma'at

George's companion Anubis, God of the Dead, forces him through the Sea of Flame as he had through all the fearful Gates of the Tuat.

At each Gate George begs him:

> Kill me now and have done I pray; I repent and throw myself on the mercy of God, however long it will take to expiate my guilt.

But Anubis never speaks.

At last he stands in the Hall of Ma'at, Goddess of Truth, before the judgment throne. Here he still hopes to escape into death and appeal to a Higher Authority for the safety of his soul. Surely he could not be at the mercy of these demons?

Osiris rises from the Judgment throne and gives way to Ptah himself, the Creator of all. Nanu, Amasis, Nitocris and Atef, all now dressed in the leopard skin robes of Anubis, stand witness.

Ammut, with dagger jaws of crocodile, strong and ferocious as a starving lion, huge as a bull hippopotamus enraged, beyond terror, stands ready to execute sentence. George falls to the floor: "Why do all this", he cries, "if you intend to condemn me?"

Osiris and Anubis turn to Ptah. At last Ptah speaks:

> The innocent Shadya passed through the Gates of Tuat and the Lake of Fire. She stood here. She accepted all of that to achieve eternal life in Osiris.
>
> Now you have denied that to her. She is no more—but worse, she is reduced to be a wild spirit, not knowing, not loving and not being loved, without name and without sustenance, but unable to cease entirely.
>
> You have destroyed the most beautiful thing I have ever made—a loving, beloved and glorious human being.
>
> There is only one sentence for one such as you. I curse you with the Creator's curse to share her fate.

George realises now what would be demanded of him.

In accordance with the law, George's heart is weighed and found heavy with sin. Ammut is released from his place.

Brindisi Port, Italy

The Times special correspondent: report for the London edition on the arrival from Port Said of the 'Osiris'

The crowd waiting to great loved ones on the dockside were subdued until the captain announced the names of the dead for whose sake the Union Flag flew at half-mast.

George Robinson and Robert Johnson, who occupied adjacent cabins, are missing. The only clues found are trails of ashes in their cabins.

Their possessions have been packed up for their executors in corded boxes, and the cabins sealed against further investigation.

Mr. Robinson's executors arrived promptly to deal with his estate. The six men in leopard skin coats occasioned some comment as they removed five large boxes.

KISS OF THE VAMPIRE

STEVE WILLIS

His teeth nibbling at her neck, she felt the first nick,
sinking deeper into his arms she feels the release of his poison.
Eyes snapping open she feels her consciousness slipping,
the poison pulsing through her veins in tune with her heartbeat.
Head falling forward onto her chest she tries to fight the lethargy,
unique tiredness in each and every sinew,
her final thought, the absent-minded motion of hand to neck.

In tortured dreams she sees them descend in unison,
mouths hanging hungrily open, ready for the blood red feast before them.
Clarity remains clouded as she stirs from her imposed slumber,
the abused wounds on her neck swollen and angry, a feint pulse in her tired mind.
 His lips no longer move but she hears every word,
"Come my Twilight Princess, come and meet thy sisters."
Mind recoiling from his hungry intrusion, she feels her humanity beginning to slip,
losing itself in the downward spiral of madness.

One final effort is all she begs,
his sickly sweet voice tries to cajole her back to his embrace.
Steeling her mind she rips the door from its hinges and steps out,
laughing hysterically at their recoil from the sun.
She feels the searing pain and embraces it,
welcoming the renewed clarity it brings
and the final smile of freedom on her ashen face.

CRIMSON BLADE
BEING
THE INAUGURAL CHRONICLE OF LUCINDA CRANE, VAMPIRE HUNTER

MIKE ADAMSON

A long leather coat and red hair drew barely a glance in 21st century Whitby, but the lithe, almost statuesque woman who wore the style warranted more than a few. She was nearly six feet tall and eyes lost in pools of darkness carried more than a hint of the things ordinary folk shied away from. To call her beautiful was an understatement, but it was an angular beauty that seemed the merest veneer concealing things best left unspoken; an animal something that simmered under the tightest possible control lest it escape and create an uncivilised scene in the lap and midst of civility.

Darkness was her place. Late afternoon plunged the Old Town into blue shadow under the mantle of black clouds flying on the wind over the Esk Valley, through which the westering sun struggled at times in bursts of angry yellow. The cold wind off the North Sea tantalised her flaming hair, bit at her neck, where she stood on the short breakwater below Tate Hill Street, alone now as the chill drove late-season day trippers indoors. The town was emptying for the day, and few, but for the Goths and others devoted to the dark and occult side of this settlement between the moors and the sea, would be abroad soon.

The salt wind brushed her face with its tang of distant lands, but she closed her eyes and let the flush of sunlight paint her eyelids deep red. She heard the lap of the tide in the harbour as the mudflats were exposed at the ebb, and rich green sea-growths and black weed clothed the docks... The evening flight of the herring gulls was a sweet chorus all around her, and she heard the throb of a fishing boat putting in.

All so normal, so perfectly sane and ordinary, yet to one who had the skill to see beyond the mundane, nothing was ordinary. She sensed the shimmer not far away of an instability portal, a heat haze, a melding of this place and some other; across the harbour something stirred, a grumble as sleep faded and the entities of the dark began to sense their time was near. The ghosts at the lighthouse, the great Blackdog, the Coach of the Dead, the hob, all the old spirits that had stalked this town for hundreds of years, as real as the first time mortal eyes beheld them. Even the black panther whose apparition had begun to wander the east side of town by night since the turn of the new century.

All this was grist for the occult mill; the woman was after bigger game this night.

With a hard smile she turned up her collar and strode off the breakwater as the sun seemed to give up unequal struggle and settled over the high moors, relinquishing the town to the arms of night. When the woman stepped through the narrow sidings onto Church Street she found shops closing up, others still with the sad neon flickers of a season gone by. The summer was well over, but business clung to life with the tenacity of a leech, and she knew across the harbour the amusement arcades would throb and flicker to empty foyers and wind-swept streets, the bizarre and unsettling air of gaiety without an audience.

Pubs did their evening trade and the Goths were raging in their strongholds of blackness, blood and torment, their fury against life flung in the face of orthodoxy. Some were superficial, attracted by the mere trappings of the subculture; others were deep indeed, nursing profound philosophies of society, identity and the passage of time. And here and there, walking among them, were other things…

He was here. Javirand the Face-Changer.

"Oh, my foe of old; tonight shall be the night", she thought as the strike of her footfalls echoed thinly in the blue evening. She walked down the centre of the old bricked road between the overhanging buildings, sensing, feeling the world around her, reaching out for his signature. As day gave way to night he would stir, soon he would wake, and hunger. She stepped aside as a car went by, a few late shoppers hurrying from doorway to doorway, and she flexed neck and shoulders, worked them subtly… Felt the weight of the curved sword that rode her back under her coat, and the bulk of her twin plastic and carbon-fibre automatics in the small of her back, sundry other items of gear. Not a lot with which to face a horror that had stalked humanity for a thousand years, but she was nothing if not confident. And experienced!

The hour was still early but the day was dying before five, and she stepped into the narrow, cosy front bar of The White Horse and Griffin further along towards Bridge Street, to order mulled wine and sit alone to watch the street through inscrutable eyes. Drinkers paused for a moment to cast a glance at her striking profile, but looked away before her green orbs could swivel to them. Dark folk were ten a penny in this town, but this one had an aura that warned folks to beware, for there was nothing sham here.

An hour and evening was thick; drinkers came and went, and streetlights glimmered on the river beyond the swing-bridge. Still none would approach her, and she felt the antipathy of their stares. "If you did but know", she thought, smiling faintly as she toyed with the last warm red velvet in her glass:

If you knew, you would crawl into your beds and shake with fear until the sun returns. And thank me with all your hearts…

Suddenly, she felt the vampire wake. Like shattering icicles, a thrill of otherworldly recognition shot through her mind and she felt his first intake of breath. It made no difference what face he wore in this place and time; she would know his mind-spoor. He was close, less than half a mile away, she had tracked him here when she first felt him stirring from his long slumber, and now she would finish it.

The last warm, spiced wine passed her red lips, then her black-gloved fingers turned the glass over on the table before her as she rose in a swirl of leather and stepped out, jerking a zip to her throat against the chill. Eyes followed her back as she went, and she turned towards Bridge Street, drawing from her deep pocket a soft, folded hat, which she opened out and flexed to shape, a broad brim against the night-time cold.

The bridge was closed, the odd car went by, and she saw diners in the fish restaurants, the warm glimmers from the bar of The Dolphin. She followed Church Street West, feeling for her prey, and at last stood in the glow of streetlights by the small boat berths, sniffing the night air. She could hear a ceilidh band playing softly from a tavern along the way, and saw huge brown gulls settled to sleep on posts and bollards… So peaceful, so normal, but she knew there would be blood this night and maybe soon.

"Where are you?" she whispered, turning slowly on the spot, eyes closed. "Where are you hiding, old friend?"

A drawn-out baying answered her from somewhere high above; she smiled thin as a razor, for only she had heard that ethereal sound. The Blackdog they called the Barguest Hound objected to more company on his crowded turf, and called from the East Cliff with a warning. She crossed the street, found the ancient stone steps of Caidmon's Trod and began to trace her way up between the tall houses, past where the old ship chandlers' shops and the rope-works used to stand in centuries gone by, following the walk toward the halls above and the sacred headland.

"How like him to hide near holy ground", she thought as she rose above the town and soon looked down on its roofs: "Mask his psychic scent with the resonance of prayer… But where could he be?"

She paused to catch her breath, looked back at the lights of the town shimmering on the languid river, and felt the bite of the wind. This was his sort of night, and some late reveller on these ancient streets would pay a terrible price—maybe… It was also her sort of night, and she smiled like a death's head as she felt the wind tug at the hems of her long coat and play in her hair. She smelled the salt, listened to the night… The town was quiet below, its lights a sad reminder of campfires in the dark, that crucible of humanity where language, story and legend had been born, long ago. Mortals still huddled around their flames to hide from overarching nature, and the woman nodded with a maternal understanding of those needs.

The Barguest Hound bayed once more and she looked up to find the first silver of moonrise over the North Sea, a waning disc just past full that lit the cloudscapes in ethereal glimmers and stroked the salt-melted stone of the old Abbey's naked bones. Yes! The vampire was awake and hungry… She hurried on along the beaten trail, through the rank grass of early winter toward the long stone wall backing the old coach houses of the Abbey house complex. He was close, she felt, as she walked on toward the glimmers of St Mary's Church against the angry evening sky, and found herself at last on Church Lane, the footpath that became Abbey Lane and wound south around the skeletal remains of the abbey itself.

There was no service tonight, and the graveyard was deserted, the wind playing like an insane piper among the leaning stones. So many psychic resonances dwelled in this place, their interplay was almost more than her higher senses could stand and she knew it placed her at a disadvantage. "Of course he chose this spot, he is nothing if not experienced", she thought; but with every moment the chances of her finding his lair before he went forth into the night to slake his demon-thirst grew slimmer, and she scowled. The best she might do was intercepting him at his carnage, or trail him back from there…

She stood still in the blustering wind and closed her eyes, stretched out and found only the confused melee of spoors… The Blackdog was by here often; the Coach of the Dead had circled this graveyard times without number… All left their traces and this headland was a maze of glowing filaments leading to and from eternity. All she could do was keep watch; sure she would know when he moved.

She vaulted the dry stone wall and settled in the lee of a corroded, ancient gravestone, drew her coat close with collar up, to bring out her twin automatics and with precise motions screw into place silencers, check the actions, load and safety each weapon. They went into deep pockets that formed discrete holsters and then she brought out the sword and laid it across her knees, gloved hand light on the braided hilt. And waited…

Deep in her listening trance, the hours went by and she felt the vampire's caution, his arrogance, his anger. He was hungry now, but he was aware of her as surely as she of him, and he knew he would not pillage unchallenged this night. "Come on, you thing of hate", she mused to herself, "come on, try your luck…"

With twenty minutes before the pubs closed, he moved. She felt him emerge from the background noise of the place like a dark battering ram. He cleared the wall of the coach-yards a hundred yards away and she was up, vaulted the wall and ran in a crouch, sword in hand. She knew better than to look for him; he was too swift, too dark… He crossed the fallow land of the cliff's shoulder, raced across the open grasses, passed Caidmon's Trod and with a vampire's inhuman ease took flight in a springing bound to the rooftops behind the Blackhorse Yard, bounded from one to another, then dropped in a plummet into the yard of the hotel.

Breath catching in her throat, the avenger repeated the feat, boots striking the red roofing tiles in precisely the same places and then felt the rush of wind as she dropped to a smashing impact in the yard, flagstones cracking as if under a hammer. Her quarry was already gone, but now she could track him. The sword went back under her coat and she was out of the yard onto Church Street before a door could be thrust open to investigate.

    A tall, powerful figure stalked towards Bridge Street and she went in pursuit, hands in pockets on the grips of her weapons, closed the gap as he turned right, and broke into a run in the shadows. When she turned he was half way across the bridge, moving with the economical tread of the powerful. Any watching from the door of the Dolphin as closing time approached saw only a Goth stalking the streets of his beloved night, all cloak and pale face, and let him be, his world was his own, and in that willing anonymity was his license and mandate to take his needs.

"Not if I have any say."

    She settled to trail him at a discrete fifty yards; he looked back just once as he turned right on St Anne's Staithe, and she caught a flash of dark smile from a hard face beneath wind-blown hair… Whatever form he wore this time he could never deceive her, and her palms itched to draw the pistols and send him into the harbour in a hail of shot—but more definite, and indeed satisfying, methods were required to rid the world of his sort. He strolled along the harbour front, past the closed-up rock-candy stores and Goth boutiques, restaurants and curio shops, and hooked left at the Marine Café. When she lost sight of him she broke into a run, knowing he would be opening the gap, and when she turned he was nowhere to be seen. His spoor had moved on up the West Cliff, and she took the route by the Seaman's Mission Cafe, up through crumbling stone steps, across a car park and onto Cliff Street. Nothing…

    He was a way on to the west, his scent fading, and she summoned her strengths, breathed deeply, then ran cat-footed along Cliff Street, turned at a private driveway, bolted through gardens behind the tall houses and cleared a wall in a graceful leap that saw her on the open commons off Silver Street. From there she was a blur of motion, clearing the opposite fence and taking the side street beside West Cliff Congregational Church. She came to a halt in the middle of Belle Vue Terrace, panting softly.

    The feel of his presence was almost a violation, as if he was stroking her body with his pallid hands, and she turned in a half-crouch, looking one way and another … until her perception drew her eyes upward, up, up the old stonework of the church, to the lead-tile roof and spire. She saw nothing but he was up there, and she drew stealthily into the shadows of a side street. The clock at the bottom of Belle Vue was grazing midnight.

"Time, gentlemen, please," was the publican's cry since time immemorial as the clock struck twelve, and she heard drinkers leaving the Granby in ones and twos, just around the corner. She had the overwhelming impression that Javirand was marking his victim even then, and she eased the pistols into her palms in her pockets, thumbed the safeties off, and stepped into the blue wash of the street lights, every nerve on fire.

A couple of Goths left the pub and nodded a courteous greeting to what they believed was one of their own, and in that moment of distraction she lost her lock on her quarry. In a terrible rush of what seemed dark wings, a cloud of grey nothingness dropped from the church spire and seemed to envelope a young tourist who had stepped out as the pub door was closed. The young woman had not even time to cry out before she was swept up in that ball of darkness and sucked into the air.

Pistols presented, the red avenger fought to draw a line of fire but her quarry was gone in the blink of an eye, and she broke into a headlong run back the way she had come, tracking him by the red balefire of his psychic malevolence. Up and over the church—but he could not maintain this energy output for long, he needed to strike, drink, and recover strength...

The vacant lot: she ran with her pistols drawn, skated around behind the church and cleared the fence in one bound, but the sight that greeted her stopped her short. She was far too late, the body was in ruins, a scarlet mess where the throat had been, clutched almost lovingly in the arms of the thing Javirand had become.

It was white as a worm, humanoid but other than human; massive thews were tipped with vicious claws, eyes blazed like red witch-fire. Blood dripped from massive fangs, and in the dim wash of streetlights the thing leered, unafraid.

"Lucinda Crane, my old enemy," came the words, growled deep in the huge throat. "When will you lose your pity for these mortals and live up to your potential?"

For a long, terrible moment she met his eyes over her open sights from a crouch twenty feet away, and then he laughed and vanished in a swirl of grey vapour through which her rounds passed harmlessly.

She closed her eyes in the anguish of defeat and knew she had to move, the last thing she needed was to be connected to the worst murder in Whitby's history... But when she reopened them she saw something she had never expected.

A blue aura hung over the body, pulsing softly, and in the wash of radiance shapes moved... Insectoidal, like locusts the size of dogs, the creatures worked methodically, digging like sexton beetles but opening not a grave but a portal between realities. One of the hobs glanced at her, seemed to fix her with an otherwordly stare, then redoubled its efforts, and the mutilated corpse settled through the torn sward until it vanished from sight. The hobs swept the grasses all around with their raking fingers, and then drew the earth back together seemingly as it had been before. Their chitinous jaws chittered in triumph and they faded with the blue light.

It was a disappearance the Police would never solve; one of the hundreds, thousands, of cases reported but never closed. Crane shuddered, pocketed her guns and turned to vault the fence once more, making her way quickly from the scene. She headed south, following Silver down to Flowergate, took a left and made her way by the closed up shops down to the harbour frontage by the bridge.

Her heart was steadier now, the weight of her weapons more comforting. She stood to look up across the river to the East Cliff and smiled, thin as a blade.
"You made a mistake," she whispered. "Now that you've fed your spoor is as bright as an arc-light. You can't hide from me." With confident tread she crossed the road and took the bridge, her resolve hard as granite. He could keep moving most of the night but his breed had an Achilles heel in needing secret sanctuary in daylight.

The wind blustered, driving the clouds before it, and the silver face of the moon found the town from time to time. Lights were going out all over now, windows darkening as the streets were at last devoid of life but for the odd cat that darted from shadow to shadow, and the unseen tread of things less worldly.
Would Javirand allow her to find his lair unopposed? Certainly not, he must be secure in his secret before he closed his eyes. If she found him asleep she could take his head and stake his heart before he could react. No... He would come for her long before dawn.

The hate was an old one, the old for the new. How many times had they fought? Gloved fingers counted them off. His native India in 1865; Afghanistan, 1880; Vienna, 1886 and London 1888, back to back and nicely obscured by the unrelated Ripper case in the latter; Lisbon, 1912, Istanbul, 1915... Then a long sleep for them both and a horrifying pursuit through the misery and blood of the Eastern Front as the Germans had fallen back after the Battle of Kursk. Wherever there was blood to spare, Javirand would be there, wearing a new face each time, thirsting beyond all control, disdaining of the mortals upon whom he fed.

He had been trapped in Berlin at the time of the airlift but he had not starved, not when the citizens had been his prey. She had not even scratched him that time. New York, 1957; Hong Kong 1964, on the front door step of the world's newest and most brutal war, soaking up the flood of lost souls that sought refuge. She almost had him there, but his gorging was so great he had slept in some lost tomb for decades, emerging in a world changed by technology. For the last twenty years they had played cat and mouse, hunting by computer, calling in favours. The place changed, the tools evolved, the game never did. Kill or be killed, and her resolve had never wavered.

Indeed, as the decades had gone by, she had learned more about the vampire condition, less guided by ancient habits and superstitions and more compelled by a gathering understanding. He slept the ages between killing bouts. She chose other means of aversion and with each lull in their war became more and more certain of her allegiance to mortals.

Her own vampirism was of a very different sort. She walked in the light, ate and drank things other than blood; though her powers were far less developed than his shape shifting and teleporting, they remained superhuman. Infinite life was both a gift and a curse, as ever, but it would be less a curse when she had made her world a safer one by ridding it of an old, unwelcome competitor.

Lucinda stood in the deserted shadows of Church Street as the wind played under the eaves. All the life was gone from the town, it was as if they had stepped back centuries to an age when the frail human form was protected by no more than brick and wood from a world so vast and savage that survival itself was a moot point. Living from age to age gave her a perspective that saw in modern society a desperate scramble for identity, and in the Goth movement among which she blended a quaint and often— it seemed to her—shallow expression of the same thing. Their lives were so fleeting, so temporary, she could, however, forgive them almost any quest for meaning. She breathed the eternal salt tang of the ocean, flexed her mind and stretched out, finding the psychic flair of her quarry without difficulty. He was up somewhere high, watching, waiting.

She was content to let him come to her. After so thorough a gorging he would not feed again tonight or possibly for weeks. Her only need was to pick the ground on which they would do battle, and that was her prerogative; after all, he was the one who must retreat to his lair before the sun returned. If he lapsed into deep slumber she had all the time in the world to find him, dig him out and finish him; so he would try to finish her first, while his strengths were at their greatest.

The sun had been gone seven hours, and was seven hours away. They had plenty of time to play, and Lucinda turned to make her way slowly and purposefully along the street towards the turn to the 199 steps that wound up around the cliff to the church. As soon as she moved he would know she was coming, and snarl his pleasure, and he was welcome to come out and fight at any moment.

She rose a step at a time, smiling as she remembered the folklore that the steps could never be counted to the same number twice. The wind mounted around her and she turned up her collar, tugged her hat down more firmly, and endured the bite of the sea wind with the stoicism and endurance of her kind. She took her time, paused to sit quietly at the lookout points and let her eyes wander over the quiet rooftops, the glimmers on the river, all the while feeling the presences of the unseen. The panther was prowling tonight, somewhere in the streets, a slinking black beast of muscle and balefire eyes… The ghosts were abroad in their endless quest to break through the barrier between the worlds, and the Hound was wandering by the intermittent moonlight.

"My kind of town", Lucinda thought with the bleak humour of one whose province was eternity. When she finished the steps to the cliff top she saw the illuminated columns of the ruined abbey against the dark sky and remembered so many others—Riveaux, Selkirk, Haughmond—each with its gothic appeal, each striking, each a sad yet triumphant reminder of human travail, enduring spirit and the relentless reclamation by nature of all that human ingenuity might accomplish. What better arena for their eternal conflict?

With a measured stride she walked up Church Lane, past the graveyard toward the walls of the old abbey, and experienced the overwhelming sensation that she was being watched. He was up there on the rotted stone columns, his eyes following her every movement as she strode on by the gatehouse and into the full bite of the sea wind. She heard the roar and tumble of breakers below the cliffs, heard the wind sing in the columns that were lit by the face of the moon as the clouds parted… This was as good as any place, and she strode onto the open lawn between the cemetery and the Coastguard radio station further along Abbey Lane, turned and eased her sword free, to stand like a black statue, closed to all but the need to sense her opponent. She could do this all night if need be, her endurance and concentration unmatched by any mere mortal.

"Come to me", she mused, projecting the thought:

> Come to me and taste my steel, let us do battle as we have for a century and a half. I will end your reign of terror, as I have vowed to.

Now she was centred, grounded, and the wind and the dark lost their power. The dim wash of lights from the lane was all she needed, her pupils wide. Her sword vibrated thinly as the wind sang across its razor-honed edge, and she adjusted its angle to vary the tone, until the sword sang as if with a life of its own, thrown in defiance to the dark power above. Perhaps Javirand enjoyed the sound of the singing blade, for it bridged the ages, harking back to the times when the sword was master, a time they remembered well. They remembered the world before the coming of engines and electronics; a time when firearms were crude and the measure of the warrior was somewhat different. She imagined him sitting up there on the towers somewhere, eyes closed, head moving softly as he was transported back by that ethereal tone, and in that simple sharing she knew, with a sense of faint revulsion, that they had more in common with each other than either had with mortals.

"Why do you love them?" Javirand had asked, long ago. It was 1915, in Istanbul, when they had fought on the rooftops of the Grand Bazaar, sword to sword, as the Great War had worsened around them...

> Why do you love them so? What makes them more worthy of your allegiance than your own kind?

Her only answer had been compassion: hers for mortals who were trapped in a single lifetime, and theirs for each other and the good they were capable of. He had snorted in derision and mentioned the war, and she had shrugged and laid him open from sternum to groin. The fight had been bold and bloody, he had sliced her to the bone, but they had disengaged when the Turkish police had swarmed the rooftop. She had healed with the same sort of speed as he, a day and even the scars were gone.

As she now stood in the North Sea wind and waited, she meditated upon his term, "your own kind". In the near-hundred years since he had spat those words at her, she had often thought of them. There were more vampires in the world than anyone imagined, lineages and allegiances, houses and cliques, tribes and clans, all interwoven through thousands of years of secretly-recorded history; history that lived best in the memories of those who had been there and yet endured. Two great lines had emerged, those whose mutation—for mutation was all it could possibly be —imprisoned them eternally in darkness, raging in their cold fury against the world, outcast and proud in the terror they inspired and those whose mutation was of a different sort, one which was far less susceptible to the effects of full frequency light, and whose digestion was not disengaged from general biological matter. Yes, she drank blood, she metabolised whole blood as part of her necessary life process, but over the years had cultivated a taste for O-negative in a martini glass, over ice. It was less primal than the hunt, and the likes of Javirand considered it weakness, but it made for a far easier blending with the mortal world from which they had originally come; and a much readier understanding of it, even affection...

Thus, her allegiances; she was not the only one of her kind who fought on behalf of the mortals, and her convictions had not been found wanting. Humankind was a beast capable of scaling sublime heights or wallowing in unspeakable depths, and all was bland unity on a universal scale, but vampire kind dwelled not among the stars but upon a single living world, and sometimes sides had to be taken. She had chosen hers long ago.

Javirand came at her like a whirlwind, a flurry of formless vapour that solidified into the worm-white killing apparition, dropping out of the dark as he cleared the abbey walls in his descent from the crumbling towers above. Speed was his greatest asset, he hit the ground in a crouch, sprang like a great cat and his claws whistled over her head as she dropped on one knee and her sword wove a tapestry of moonlight. Now the song of air over the honed edge was a devil's wail as she moved like lightning, the blade a blur of motion.

None in the sleeping town would believe this drama was playing out, none would believe any glimpses caught on the CCTV covering the abbey gatehouse, and the shadows hid a conflict as old as the world. Javirand, in his combat morph, was a seven-foot killing machine able to defy gravity and teleport at will, and these gifts had made him both arrogant and predictable. Lucinda had minimal ability in the former and none in the latter, and put her faith in speed and agility as always, and the ability to defeat strength with intelligence. Her sword created a zone of exclusion around her that the dark vampire strove to defeat, to get through with his grasping reach, any way to distract her long enough to take out her throat and then finish her at his leisure.

At last he flipped away from her a few yards and morphed back to his human guise, resting from his enormous energy output, even so panting only shallowly. The face he wore was stern, broad but not unattractive in a dark and forbidding way. His black clothing left his face no more than a pale, disembodied image in the gloom.

"Come along, Lucinda," he said pleasantly in a rich baritone, still formed around his native Indian accent:

> Much as I enjoy our infrequent wrestling matches, we both know it can only end one way. I have always been stronger and one day your luck will run out.

The woman took the almost contemptuous offer of rest stoically, her upraised blade a crescent of bright steel between them:

> What could we possibly have to talk about? Since we first fought in Jaipur there has been no quarter, nor will there ever be.
> A shame; If I could but mingle our mutations, who knows what you would become? Your powers would triple.

"My powers are fine as they are," she whispered.
"You are weak!" he snarled, arms folded on his chest. "Weak in body, mind and spirit! Compassion—" the word dripped scorn:

> ... is your nemesis. Only in ruthlessness is strength, and only in strength is survival. Our kind, yours and mine, will still walk proud upon this Earth the day the sun swells above us, but theirs...

He waved a hand abstractly at the town below:

... they will be dust. Blown on the winds of hell, and rightly forgotten for the vermin they are.

"Vermin from which we are descended!"
"Evolved! We are the next step, they are obsolete! They are to us as the monkey is to them!" After a long moment he waved a hand in dismissal. "Enough. Lucinda, has it never occurred to you that I would sooner turn you than kill you?" He smiled faintly, letting his words hang on the night wind. He studied his fingertips for a moment:

> I might have killed you a hundred times over the years, but what a waste that would be. To elevate you to the ranks of my own kind, what a force you would become. Tell me you do not wish to feel *real* power?

The last was said almost seductively.
Her voice was a gravelling purr, her eyes like black coals:

> We are worlds apart. The greatest rush of power I will ever feel will be the satisfaction when your head leaves your shoulders.

He shook his head sadly:

> Not this time, then. The more strength I waste the sooner I must drain another of your despicable mortals. So, enough!

He shrugged, threw his arms wide and vanished in a swirl of grey vapours.
For a long, difficult moment, Lucinda stood panting, eyeing the dark over her blade. She reached out psychically; stretched for his signature and realised he was nowhere near. Some distance away now, under cover, hidden away. He need never expose himself, but walk through walls to leave and return. There was solid stone between them, and the status was quo.

She returned her blade to its scabbard under her coat with slow, practiced actions, her mind racing to process his words. Had he really been playing with her all these years? Or was he bluffing, because she really had his back to the wall this time?

The night was undisturbed, their battle had gone unnoticed, and in truth it had been only a few minutes in length. She jogged to the cemetery and vaulted the dry stone wall, to crouch in the lee of a gravestone and marshal her thoughts. Should she walk away this time? Leave his playing field open, let more unsolved murders stain this town, then track him down for an eleventh time somewhere, somewhen, else?

"I am weary of this game", she thought, "I want it over, now".

She gathered her thoughts, her spirit and her strengths around her, and found a thread of her vampire being envying Javirand the hot, fresh blood he had supped so deeply upon not long ago. For all her compassion, she was what she was; a predator that could never wholly cease to be what nature had made her. She thrust it aside; she had the strength to finish this business before finding her own nourishment in the least traumatic way.

The clock tower of the church showed 2am, and she was surprised by the passage of time. Her wide pupils saw the world in greys and greens, silver and deepest blues, not darkness but a rich palette, and she wrapped her coat against the chill air of night.

She had studied Whitby and its occult traditions in great depth before embarking on this mission, and she knew intimately the history of this headland. It had been home to the first wooden abbey in the 7th century, and, until her death in 680, to the abbess St. Hilda, whose ghost still walked and was seen between the towers in luminous majesty. She had hosted the Synod of Whitby in 664, which fixed the dating of Easter. The original abbey was razed by the Vikings in 851, rebuilt in stone by a Norman knight in the 11th century, and came to its end in 1540 in the great Dissolution under Henry VIII. The Church of St Mary was more recent, the earliest structures dated from 1110, though most of what existed in the present day was 18th century, especially the interior. The famous cemetery with its salt-corroded stones hosted many a seaman's remains, and the seafaring tradition of the town had it that a coach of the dead welcomed newly buried sailors by circling the grave three times and collecting the soul of the departed for a proper seaman's repose among his own kind. The last burial here had been the very year she had first fought her nemesis, and part of the cliff edge had recently broken away in heavy rains, spilling ancient bones into Henrietta Street, below...

That was the Sunday-school version of the headland's history, she knew many another tale, and she sat to brood upon them as the hands of the clock wound away the minutes. She remembered a story, a tale of the time when Captain Browne Bushell, lord of Bagdale Hall, across the river, and whose ghost still prowled the manner to this day, had fought first for one side, then the other, during the English Civil War. The mid-17th century was a brutal time, of immolation and pitch-capping, of racking and gouging, and it was said that a party of Parliamentarians had spent several weeks creating an escape tunnel on this headland, having discovered, by the serendipitous collapse of a part of the old abbey grounds many years before, a series of chambers that had been part of the foundations of the 11th century structure. They had dug a tunnel into those chambers to use as a hiding place from Royalist forces, should push come to shove, and could retreat into them at a moment's notice. The entrance, according to the story, was through a grave in the cemetery of St Mary's, consecrated but empty.

What would be more cynical than for Javirand to secrete his physical remains in a chamber beneath the sanctified soil that would otherwise be deleterious to him?

The oldest graves were no longer legible in terms of inscriptions, the salt wind had corroded the stone, turning smooth-worked tablets into rippled layers of chemical-stained rock, leaning and falling into disarray. Among the vertical tablets were many other designs, including pillar and altar tombs, and some of these were also very old. She knew the approximate location of the oldest surviving tombs, and if the chambers in the abbey foundations were the object then it was unlikely the entrance was in any grave on the side adversely affected by landslides in the intervening centuries.

She was in fact almost on top of the site, right where she crouched. She took from a pocket a thermal scope and switched it on, put it to one eye and swept the gravestones around her. Equal heat values returned a mosaic across the cold grasses, stone after stone, and she walked slowly along the ranks of graves, scanning the oldest, most weathered. At last she stood by an early modern period altar tomb, its stone weathered so severely it seemed almost a natural boulder, and registered a slight difference in the temperature of the stone, as if airspace behind it conducted heat at a different rate from the dense earth of the others.

Returning the scope to her pocket, she let her night vision correct itself gradually, then felt the stone with a brushing touch of her gloved fingers. She put an ear to the smooth, cold slab and rapped hard, listening to the quality of the echo... Yes, it was hollow beneath. That in itself meant nothing, many tomb graves were sepulchural chambers containing a freestanding coffin. She would not know until she had done what was necessary.

For a human it would have been impossible, no matter what was seen in movies. The cover stone weighed at least five hundred pounds, and only the inhuman strength of one such as she could have moved it unaided and without tools. The slab shifted grudgingly and emitted a draft of stale air, and she noted how carefully it had been fitted to its supports. It was meant to deflect water from reaching the interior, and certainly there seemed minimal water damage when she put a penlight into the tomb and flicked the beam on. The chamber was empty, around four feet deep and lined with smoothly-cut stone, and at one end steps disappeared down into total blackness.

Now she steeled her courage. This was entering the real night, this was the monster's world, and though her resilience would bring her through any ordinary trial, to fight the beast in this narrow space had both advantages and drawbacks. She dropped into the hole and used her shoulders to ease the stone back into place, then crouched and used the thermal sight once more. The steps led downward for maybe ten feet, curiously unworn as if they had never known human tread and her footfalls were a thin echo as she stepped into a tunnel whose roof caused her to stoop. It ran off straight into the blackness, and now she brought out a single pistol to cover the night ahead... and moved slowly into an icy stillness that seemed to have evaded all passage of time.

Slowly, slowly… there was no rush. There was only cold stone behind her; all the threat in her world was to the fore. The thermal sight showed her a uniform grade of heat from floor to ceiling as the soil temperature varied with depth, and she fought to make out anything of use. She could switch to flashlight or even a flare, but to her wide pupils it would be like staring into the sun, destroying her night vision. Even her eyes would take several minutes to reset, a mortal's would take hours, but even minutes would be far longer than Javirand needed to do his work.

His implicit threat to turn her was a knot of fear on her belly. She had no idea what the result would be of mixing the two vampire strains, and did not want to be the test subject to find out. She just wanted to find him and finish the job, one surgical stroke of her blade was all it would take to immobilise him and then his immortality would become his living hell.

The tunnel reached on ahead, a silent vault. She knew he was somewhere out there, in the old basements of the abbey, his psychic spoor was bright at this distance, and its modulation told her he was probably already asleep. The penalty of his powers was exhaustion, and in his complacency he may not have designed to research the mere human doings of this place. He could in fact be oblivious of the existence of this tunnel. "Give him time to settle into deep slumber", she thought, easing down to kneel on the hard flagstones. She set down her pistol and sought her flashlight, felt for the switch and lit only a single LED, shielded her eyes from it and peered down the arched stone way in what seemed a sudden blue-white brilliance. It was clear to a wooden partition maybe fifty yards ahead, and she crept on slowly, her noise-discipline at its greatest.

At the door she killed the LED, put the thermal scope to her eye and scanned the joints between vertical planks that seemed hoary with age. There was a definite temperature increase in the chamber beyond and she played the scope along each division between the boards, looking for anything she recognised beyond.

Nothing… She listened for a long while but no sound came to her keen ears. After a time, she used the single LED and examined the partition. It seemed less a door than simply a barricade, fitted into the mouth of the tunnel, probably a last line of defence should the hideaway be found. She would have expected it to be barred, but that presupposed Javirand was aware of the tunnel and this chamber. The abbey had many basement rooms, a tradition told of a young nun walled up alive for adultery in one of them… After careful inspection, she slid a knife from a boot sheath and probed through the gaps in the ancient boards, slid both up and down, and encountered no horizontal bars. Now she smiled wolfishly: she had a chance.

She set her shoulder to the wood and drew a deep breath, focussed, then began to exert her superhuman strength. She felt the timbers creak as the first new force was applied to them in 360 years. She went slowly and carefully, changed her position and the angle of thrust, and gradually felt the mass of oak begin to move. It grated against the stone around it, dust trickled down the walls, and she kept up the pressure, one boot against the wall for leverage. If the timber shifted suddenly and fell to the floor her element of surprise would be gone, so she must in fact catch it before that could happen.

To switch from pushing to pulling in a split second, in near total darkness, was likely beyond a mortal, but not a vampire, and when the moment came she rebalanced in the blink of an eye, snaked a hand around the edge of the massive panel and stabilised it as it swayed. At once the psychic impact was doubled, this lost lair had been imbued with his essence for some time now, and she concentrated to block out the foul feeling... Now she could ease the barricade aside and step through, and the LED showed her a stone flagged chamber in which were stacked boxes and barrels—gunpowder and flints, pistol balls, packages of food long since decayed. Muskets leaned against a wall, and the ages fell away as she imagined the last hands to have filled this store room, so long ago.

On the other side of the chamber was a heavy, iron-bound timber door of Medieval design, arched at the top. On cat-like tread she stepped through the dust of ages, LED extinguished, and put the thermal sight to her eye at the dry-rotted gap around the great planks.

And froze...

Heat bloomed in her eyepiece and she saw part of a humanoid form, stretched out on a pedestal of crates and tarpaulin... The few things he had teleported into this place for his meagre needs. He may choose to live in luxury elsewhere but prided himself on his Spartan virtue when hunting and he slept his otherworldly trance without need of comforts. She saw his breath plume in the chill air, a long, slow exhalation, his metabolism slowed...

She examined every rotten gap, searched for the right perspective, observing Javirand where he lay about ten feet away. He had never been so much at her mercy; she had never located his sleeping place before. The monster was vulnerable, and in this closed space she had suddenly become the beast, the hunter.

The massive old door was dry-rotten, its timbers were five centuries old at least, and she knew she could break them by force, but it was a question of time. He could wake far quicker than she could break. The barrel-hinges would be rusted into place, they would squeal like banshees, assuming they would swing at all... If it was all about speed, she had only so many options, and stepped back to gently place the LED light on a shelf in the store room and draw out her automatics.

She removed the magazine from one and replaced it with another whose rounds were colour-coded red: explosive shot. She left one standard round in the chamber above the explosive rounds, with the weapon primed to cycle from the open bolt position. Then she thrust the second pistol into her belt, drew her sword, and began to breathe deeply, cycling her oxygen level, before extinguishing the LED and going to one knee at the door, silencer to the crack between the boards and thermal scope balanced over the sights…

The squit of the silenced round was painfully loud in the deathly silence, and she saw a burst of heat that obscured all else, but from the sound of the tumbling body she knew she had been on target, the shot cleanly through the brain pan. That in itself would not kill a vampire, but it would certainly slow him down long enough, and she flicked the LED on full, to step back and thumb the pistol selector to full auto. The entire magazine ripped free in a braying snarl, a flicker of muzzle flame, as she tracked an arc. The pattern of detonations filled the air with flying splinters and bits of flame, and when she hurled her weight at the door the timbers burst inward in a collapsing chaos. She went through, dropped the weapon and snatched the other free, to hurl herself over Javirand's sleeping pallet…

The body was not on the floor…

She looked up in the harsh contrast of the flashlight beam in time to see him morphing into his hunter form, the gaping wound in the side of his head closing as she watched. His snarl was loud as thunder in the closed chamber, his thews swelling to herculean proportions as his rage magnified, and when she raised her other pistol he laughed in her face.

"You are less than pathetic," he snarled:

> How many times will you try the same thing and expect a different outcome? Why are you incapable of learning?

He flexed his huge hands: "And now I shall turn you."

Lucinda's eye looked over the open sights, calm and clear, and she was almost regretful as she savoured the moment. "Oh, I can learn," she said softly, and triggered a single round. The rosette of blood over his heart should have meant nothing, but at once the towering apparition staggered back against the wall, pawing at its breast, an expression of dawning horror contorting its terrible features. "What…?" he whispered. "What have you… done?"

Lucinda pumped two more rounds into his chest, dropped the weapon and hefted her sword, danced in closer than she had ever dared and thrust with all her might. The razor-honed blade went through the great, pallid body and nailed him to an ancient timber; she whirled and collected the pistol once more.

His eyes were desperate, pain wracking him now, and wisps of smoke rose from the gaping chest wounds. "What have you done?!" He roared, great hands now seizing the blade and working at it—though she saw his strength was failing fast. In moments more he was unable to sustain his form and returned to his human guise, a now almost pitiable spectacle of a man impaled and dying, an ironic tribute to old Vlad himself, whose hideous exploits in the 15th century had inspired Bram Stoker to write his classic novel in this very town.

Lucinda stepped nearer as his flesh began to smoulder:

> These are wooden bullets, they shatter on impact. They were lathed from the wood of a sanctified cross, and carry a silver dart inside them. It makes no difference if I believe in such antiquated things, but if you do … Ahhh.

She winked one dark eye. "That was a 21st century staking. Enjoy eternity dead."

His eyes widened with knowledge of impending death, of his total and ultimate failure, and a hand pawed the air before him. One last desperate defiance was thrown at the fates from slack and drooling lips: "My brothers will avenge me….!"

She snapped up the weapon and emptied the rest of the magazine through him, and as he burst into flames she wrenched her sword free of wall and chest. He collapsed to his knees and she drew back for a massive stroke that took his head off cleanly.

In the balefire of the reaction, as vampire flesh was consumed by the conflicting energies, she stepped back, put up a hand to shield her eyes, and wrinkled her nose at the offensive odour. It was over in moments, the entire body, head included, shrivelling in a wreath of gold-green flame that heated the chamber as it had never know before, and then faded away… A pile of white ash collapsed upon itself.

Silence… The glare of the LED flashlight was the only energy left, his psychic trace was at last gone from the world, and Lucinda sank heavily upon his sleeping platform, to pant, shoulders heaving as the reality of her victory finally asserted itself.

They had warred for 143 years. Suddenly she felt lonely—what would her world be without him? But a smile crept through a moment later, Peaceful—Cleaner. That was what it would be. And he was hardly the only dark vampire; she did not discount his warning, but it took many years for the affairs of vampire-kind to unfold, and by the time his siblings and comrades knew anything of this sad tableau under the sanctified sod of the ancient headland, she would have found newer pastures.

Abruptly the world was again worth living in, and she cleaned her blade with slow care before sheathing it with a decisive thrust, and retrieving her pistols. The way out was clear before her and she eased the grave slab slowly aside with a feat of strength to emerge into the cold sting of the night wind ten minutes later. She squared up the slab and stood in the dark to look up at the abbey, feel the ages flowing about her, hear the plethora of ghosts and spirits, entities and beasts that boiled through the dimensions in this focal place, and she smiled softly.

This was a new century, a time of new beginnings and new directions. Vampire-kind had survived for thousands of years, and would accompany mortals into the future, but its place as ever would be one of shadows. She squared her shoulders, looked up at the flying clouds before the westering moon, and vaulted the stone wall to make her way down the 199 steps, a slow strike of boots on stone that told sleeping residents' subconscious minds that this was a town that never really, fully, slept.

She would watch the sun rise over the North Sea in a silver-pink wash as the herring gulls took flight, and when the first pubs opened their doors she would take a breakfast of mortal food, and enjoy it. But as she sat on the breakwater below Tate Hill Street, among sleeping seabirds, she could not help sensing that siren song of her own reality, and acknowledging that her battle had left her hungering—really hungering, not for mere food, but for the sustenance of her kind, that strange ambrosia that would forever force her to walk apart from the humans she respected. She needed blood; warm, fresh, human blood. When the day was begun and she would disturb no one, she would take out her mobile and punch a well-called number.

The difference between the dark vampires and those who walked in the light, was that the latter's victims were perfectly willing.

And thus, not victims at all!

MEMENTO MORTI

COLIN YOUNGER

It is said that confession is good for the soul:

Bless me Father for I have sinned; it has been one day since my last confession and I accuse myself.
I have told lies;
I have told tales;
I have been cheeky to my parents;
I have abused myself, (I always enjoy that one; it shocks the priest);
I have sold my soul to the devil and
I have been lazy.

Perhaps I should have saved the self-abuse till last. It's always a good one for shock value. The priest composes himself; I can't see him but I know the routine.
"Do you know what you're saying, my son"? he says.

Does anybody? Wrong response; he wants me to be contrite, they all want me to be contrite; the nurses, the doctors, the officers of the law. But to be contrite you have to feel guilt, and I don't...

Let me tell you a story. Whether it is true or not is matterless. It's based on my memories, my reminiscences. Memory is an unstable animal. And of course they say I'm mad...or evil. I'll leave you to decide... I want to invite you into my wilderness; my desert.

Are you scared?

Whether you continue reading is entirely your choice. This is your get-out clause; this is your chance to say 'no' or you could say 'yes.' I said 'yes'; it changed my life. For better or worse; that's a matter of opinion.
So 'yes' or 'no?'
If 'no' I take my leave of you.
If 'yes'; read on!
My Psychiatrist Mr Cavanagh is a very nice man. He gets me to talk about myself without judging me or asking any leading questions. Here's an example:

Him: How have you been Morti?
Me: Very well Mr Cavanagh.
Him: Anything you want to discuss? Any problems?
Me: No problems; can we discuss me being the Antichrist?
Him: We can talk about why you think you are the Antichrist…

He cannot show that he believes me in any way because that would be "reinforcing an aberrant behaviour".

When they caught me the police had a different approach; quite aggressive, quite unnecessarily aggressive as far as I'm concerned…

The postman has just arrived, the postmark says 6th June 1972 and the dogs are going spare…

"Mortimer", yells Mother, "there's a letter from a solicitors' firm for you. You'd better not be in any trouble."

"Beautiful, this marmalade" I say.

"I'm glad you approve Son" smiles Mother accepting the change of subject quite readily, "although since making it I've realised that I should have used Seville oranges and a lemon. I'd never win the County competition the way it stands, but as long as you like it. Anyway what's your letter about?"

"Nothing much Mother" I lie, not wishing to give anything away, "it's just to do with my inheritance." I know that this is a sore subject but not as contentious as the truth is.

It's not my fault after all, that Great Aunt Philomena hasn't decided to leave her worldly goods to Mother. I'm not the one who caused the great debate. She was invited to the reading of the Will but declined the invitation.

"Morti", she says, "what's this all about?" "You know I need help with the housekeeping and I could pay off the mortgage with what you've been left. And where did she get it from …and…and…why you?"

"I know Mother" I protest, "but I told you what was said, I'm not allowed to give any of the money away or I lose it all."

> Well that's a fine way to treat the Mother who's looked after you all these years. So I'm to stay a pauper while you waltz around with the nouveau riche doing what you want without a care in the world?

"I'm sorry Mother" I say, although I was feeling got at really.

I lie back on my bed inhaling the mixture of scents provided by the freshly starched sheets and the emanations which have been produced by my own bodily secretions in the form of sweat.

At that the door springs open and the now menacing figure of Mother leers at me defying me to exist:
"Look at you lying there thinking that the world owes you a living" she spits. "Do you think you're clever? And if you think you're going to live under my roof for one more minute then you've got another think coming!"
"But Mother", I falsely protest, "I didn't write the Will; it's not my fault."
"Oh really" hisses Mother:

> ... and I don't suppose it was you who sat night after night with Great Aunt Philomena using her loneliness to get what you wanted. How on earth did I ever raise a child to be so manipulative, scheming and... and... evil?

I feel angry that she thinks she is responsible for my elevated state. He Who Wills raised me to this, not her.
"It's not my fault", I yell, "It's not fair; it's just not right. I don't even want her stinking money." I do, though; I am just playing along with Mother's pathetic, little games.
The door swings open again:

> Words... just words; you very much know that I can't have anything. The solicitor says that if you don't accept the provisions of the Will the proceeds are to go to... what was it? Oh I can't remember but it certainly won't go to the family. Well I hope you're pleased with yourself. Now pack your bags and get that lazy excuse for a body out of my sight and out of my life; and good riddance!

So I do.
Are you impressed by how acute my memory is; how I remember the smells, the sights and what it felt like when I was human? I remember everything. Here's another one:
"Death", said the Priest "is not the end but a transition. It is a normal part of life; a gateway to our real lives in the next world".
I love the way people talk about death without talking about it. It's almost as if they believe that if you say the word it will come and get you. Trying to evade death is picking a fight with someone you can't beat. It will win in the end.
"Doesn't she look at peace" was how my Mother described the corpse of Aunt Philomena;
"Not a wrinkle" says one of the black-clothed mourners;
"She's gone to a better place and she's happy now"; another glorious cliché from another none-person.
Funerals are fabulous things to the people-watcher. They all process in; complete the ritual goodbyes, all of them to a person thinking, "I'm glad it's not me".

Aunt Philomena's funeral was much like any funeral. She was brought in, dutifully wept over and carted off to a better place. There were the obligatory murmurs about what a good person she was in life, (she wasn't), and how stunned I must have been when she left everything to me, (I wasn't). Most people thought she had left about enough to cover the funeral expenses. I knew better, or I thought I knew better if her ramblings were anything to go on. As it happens I was right. I did know better.
"What I am leaving to you is beyond any monies", she had told me just before she died, "Only if you say 'yes', can I move on. Will you say 'yes', Morti?"

I said 'yes'.

She moved on.

Here at the funeral they know I said 'yes' and they hate me for it. I don't know what I have said 'yes' to, but it was to something and when you have nothing, something seems a very appetising proposition.

"Never trusted banks or building societies; they're all crooks always charging you for services they haven't provided" she'd confided in me. "I keep what's mine under the floorboards, and if you say 'yes' it's all yours. Everything I have".

'Yes' I said

"You are the only one who believes me, Morti said Aunt Philomena, "and so I shall leave you the means to cope with what is to be done". Could you have said 'no' to something as cryptic and enigmatic as that?

I said 'yes'.

I said 'yes' to the bifocaled solicitor too when he requested, "If you could please sign and date at the three points highlighted, Mr. Goodman I would be most grateful and then all matters may be finalised."

I said 'yes'.

To be honest I was more interested in the legs of his cheaply clad secretary, partly hidden behind a yukka plant. I did have a sex drive then. Not anymore. Had she asked me for sex I would have said 'yes'. I did imagine the scenario. Shagging her would have been quite a pleasurable diversion. I was human then. That was before my world darkened, (though it was a most illuminating darkness). That was before I was given the cash box. That was before I moved Frekka on. Had I known what I know now would I have said 'no'? No, I would have said 'yes'.

You're wondering about the cash-box aren't you? You want to know what's in it. You want me to tell you it had some kind of treasure in. It did! But your puny human minds could never comprehend the worth of the contents. Mine didn't; now it does. To understand you would have to be me and you're not. So stay in your comfortable ignorance and I'll tell you about Frekka.

Frekka didn't have a funeral but he does have a grave. His Headstone reads:

Philomena Goodman
Born 1910
Died 1972
Rest in Peace

Names are funny things. The name I was given in this world is 'Morti Goodman.' I wonder if that made me who I am. Morti as in death; Goodman as in 'Good man.' Is the good man dead in me or did he ever exist? I've had many names.

Frekka is in my room. Well, what *was* Frekka is in *this* room, which I suppose is my room now for the period of my incarceration.

"You killed me you Fucker" he says, (he always starts with that), and I always reply either 'and?', or 'so?' It gets the desired response, rage; mutely expressed but in his dead eyes, then:

"You worthless little piece of shit. Look at the state of my clothes…"

I love that. It's such an inappropriate response. Not for him though, it just shows how vain he was in life and how the bigger things didn't matter to him. Frekka the tattooed bastard from Borstal, in his pristine uniform of Crombie coat with Levi Staprest and polished brogues; I always wondered how they stayed so clean when he used them regularly to kick people's heads in. Were they shoes or weapons? Both. Not now though…

Today he is covered in filth and has a stick protruding antennae-like from his shaved head. That's covered in filth too, and blood.

"Go away, Frekka" I say. "I have things to attend to!"

Actually I have voices to attend to. They are a formidable aggravation, threatening and blasphemous, furious and impious, mocking and vicious but all of them horribly articulate. He Who Wills is the loudest and most hideously eloquent; Frekka's is the most denunciatory and vulgar…

"You killed me" he says
"No Frekka", I reply, "I moved you on!"

"I'm in Hell you little shit" he barks, "I'm in Hell and you put me here. You smashed my head in with a fucking cash box and stuck this fucking stick in my head. You carted me round town in a fucking pram and dumped me in a fucking grave. You little shit…"

My response is always the same and always gets the same reaction: 'Swearing is not big and it's not clever'. I'm not going to justify myself to a corpse or a figment of my imagination as the medics say. Besides, this glibness always makes him mad. So does this:

"Go away Frekka, I have worlds to destroy"
"You…"

Yes me, Frekka, the grammar school kid who you terrorised; the university graduate you called a ponce, the person who battered your head in with a cash box and humiliated you post-mortem.
"Go away, Frekka. I'm embarrassed by you. You look like shit, and if you smelled of anything I would imagine you would stink. Not so clever now." And with that he goes away; every time.

What do you see when you look at me? Do you see me looking back at you? Does it disconcert you? Or, do you see yourself looking at me, looking back at you? What do you see? The medics see a "paranoid schizophrenic" who suffers from "auditory and visual delusions". It wasn't always that way. In the mediaeval period I was considered a Holy Man. I was in a way, but not in the way that they thought. I wasn't aware of who I was until the letter came of course. Then I realised who I really was. He Who Wills gave me access to my special memories.

"Come on Morti, time for your medication" interrupts an insignificant.

They called me a hermit. I suppose I was. They were scared of me, (I think you might be), but they came to me for favours. Then they burned me. Strange, you would imagine pain, but there is none. Perhaps it's because of who I am. Perhaps it's because the central nervous system shuts down in shock when they pile faggots and tar at your feet and set it alight. The paradox is that you feel cold, not hot. You start to shiver and then you wake up and it's another time and another place.

"Morti, I need to roll up your sleeve."

Plague and leprosy passed me by. Usually my death has been violent and brought about by an angry mob. I've been lynched, beheaded, burned, (I mentioned that), drowned, shot and pushed off a building. Now they don't try to kill me. They sedate me. It's a sign of the times I suppose.

"Now this won't hurt; just a little scratch."

Society is not what it used to be. They have no idea of what is right and what is wrong. Scepticism has been a blessing, (paradoxical that I would use a word like that, but it's not confined to your God). I have been described as sacred and profane. Now they say I'm mad. The problem is that you people cannot apprehend abstractions: you cannot see the difference between (or even the existence of), Good and Evil.

"Now then; you'll begin to feel a little drowsy so just lie back" says the patronising white-coat.

It is very rare that one encounters sheer unadulterated evil in what you might think is a human face; an evil that is deadly, dangerous; active and all encompassing. Madness, yes you can accept that; stupidity, pride, hubris, vanity, meanness, even the crass and unnecessary violence of no-hopers like Frekka; all of these you can accept. But the truly evil in this world; you like to think they don't exist. How much easier is it to consign us to the realms of insanity? It makes you sleep better at night doesn't it?

"That's it now; you just have a nice doze."

It's very rare that you encounter real Evil in this world.

You… just have.

GREEN

Kirstie Groom

She slinks in silently,
Belly to the ground,
Slick scales shiver with anticipation,
As I, caged in my thoughts,
Remain oblivious to her advances.

She coils around my prison,
Strong and sinuous, reinforcing the
Ideas which keep me confined,
Feeding on my insecurity,
A virus, thriving as my sanity decays.

She strikes;
Fangs shred my skin, searing
Like splashes of scalding oil,
The poison spreads, turning my
blood to venomous bile.
Infected. My skin begins to shed, crumbling
Beneath my fingers, flaking away
Revealing sickly green scales.

Nothing remains, but a shrunken shadow.
I am consumed, transformed,
As she was before me.
My hair begins to writhe and hiss,
Drowning out my conscience
Which wills me to forgive.

WHERE IS SHE?

PAUL ALDERSON

*"If all we lose is the skin,
I'm putting you under within,
we're gonna make this life together."*
Richard Ashcroft

'Where is she?' he muttered.

Harry paced the floor of their living room like a caged bear, checking out of the window every time he was close to it on his circuit. He sat down and tried to watch some T.V. but found himself unable to concentrate, aimlessly flicking through channels. He got up, pacing the floor again. His gaze was drawn to their wedding photo, on the mantel piece, for the hundredth time. She was blonde and petite, he was tall and dark, and they were both grinning. He went and stood by the window like a sentry.

He worked in construction, and was generally out of the house, and back in, before her. Ellen was a teacher, and had recently started coming home late, with excuses to justify her absence; she had to give a detention, or someone had detained her in a corridor seeking a sympathetic ear, a department meeting, an extra-curricular class she had to teach, marking... He was concerned that she was avoiding him, her home life, and their situation. In the grip of his deepest fear he worried she might be cheating, but invariably she would call, or pull into the drive as his thoughts began to spiral out of control.

They had been happily married for five years, and trying for a baby for two of those, with no luck; the doctors said his sperm had low motility, and that Ellen had an inhospitable environment, which meant that their chances of conceiving were low. They decorated the spare room as a nursery. Everything was bought, and in place. They had tried everything, but every three weeks or so, they knew that they were still not pregnant. He had grown despondent, feeling like less of a man for not being able to give his wife what they both wanted, and she became by turns apathetic and hostile towards him, her body almost audibly ticking. When she was ovulating the pressure upon him was so great, that it was leaving him sporadically impotent. He was a large powerful man; years of hard work had packed his muscles solid on his thick arms, and broad shoulders. The whole thing had left him feeling emasculated, paranoid that Ellen would look elsewhere for the fulfilment she craved. He loved her so much, but sometimes his paranoia consumed him. When sex had just been for fun, he had been confident that she was his, and that he was her 'bit of rough,' assured in the knowledge that they were both satisfied, repeatedly, every night.

He called her mobile, it went straight to voicemail. She was always forgetting to charge her phone. Other worries projected in his mind; maybe she had broken down, or worse crashed. She could be stranded by the side of the road somewhere with no way to call for help. Something didn't feel right. With each scenario running on a constant loop, a memory broke through, bringing his thoughts to a halt. Harry remembered seeing a local newspaper outside the petrol station as he filled up her car, telling of another missing motorist. Fear gripped his gut, wrenching his core. He knew which way she came to and from work; it was a long way there and back, forty five minutes each way. He took her drive time into account; she was still well over an hour late, and it would be getting dark soon.

He resolved to go and find her. He went to the cupboard under the sink in the kitchen, and grabbed his torch; if he had to change a tire, or have a look at the engine, he would not do it in the dark. Its two foot length was a good, solid weight in his hands; it had a black stainless steel frame with four D-Cell batteries in it, and its beam was incredibly powerful and variable. It had been a gift from Ellen; he had been a night watchman when they first met. Her thoughtfulness was one of the reasons he had fallen in love her.

Where is she?

He grabbed his keys, left their home, and drove.

***

Ellen loved autumn; she loved the smell in the air, the way the leaves turned from green to gold to red, the way they fell; collecting here and there in drifts, blown about by the blustery wind. The wide river valley's woods and copses seemed ablaze, their varying hues marvellous, accentuated by a bright blue sky, and huge rolling white and gray cumulus clouds. Entranced by the view from her car window, she admired nature's awe inspiring splendour. It was her favourite time of year; it reminded her of that song by Nat King Cole. She started to sing the words to it:

'The falling leaves, drift by my window...'

She sang softly and sweetly as she drove, her voice clear and warm; she was thinking about pumpkin carving, and a spooky Halloween:

'But I miss you most of all, my darling...'

Her husband Harry came into her mind then, sweet lovable Harry; she missed him so much. It had been a long day, made longer because Janice had wanted to talk to Ellen about the problems Janice was having with the year ten BTEC pupils, which had digressed into the usual diatribe on school politics and Janice's numerous ailments.

Taking her usual shortcut home from work, along the deserted, back country roads, Ellen had the opportunity to think. She and Harry had not had the easiest time of it the last couple of years, things had become, a bit, mechanical between them, and she wanted to do something to ease the tension. She thought she might; take a shower, perhaps slip into something a little provocative, order takeaway, light a few candles, and open a bottle of wine. She thought that she would give him something to smile about at work tomorrow.

She noticed something blue, moving inside the shady tree line of the woods, across the field to the right. Ellen thought it must have been a boy about waist height, wearing what looked like a Lakeside school jumper, one of the feeder schools to her secondary, but Lakeside was miles from here. She couldn't really see him clearly, just the light blue of the jumper in the shadows of the trees.

What could a child from that school, be doing this far away from it?

She suddenly became very worried for the child, he was quite away off, but from what she could make out, the colour of the jumper looked marred, as if torn, or dirty. Ellen pulled the car over onto the grassy verge on the other side of the road, opened her window and shouted to the boy.

'Hey! Hey! Can you hear me? Are you alright?'

The boy stopped moving but did not turn.

'Hey! Are you okay? Are you lost?'

The cold autumn wind was gusting into her face, blowing her words away. The boy began to move further into the shade of the trees as if he had not heard her. Without thinking she got out of the car, her natural instinct to protect the child had taken over. She started to run down through the tilled field, her court shoes sinking deeply now and then into the mud, slowing her down. She had to stop a few times, to pull one or the other shoe out of the mud, and put it back on. Ellen shouted repeatedly as she ran up the sloping field to the woods to wait for her, that she was a teacher, that she could help him and not to be afraid, but she had lost sight of him.

Ellen stopped running when she got to the edge of the trees, and held on to a trunk while she gasped for breath. Her clear blue eyes searched the shadows of the wood's interior for sight of the boy. She caught a flash of blue, deep in the trees, and thought she could hear him whimpering and moaning. Ellen cried out again to him to wait as she plunged into the wood after him, imploring him to comeback, so she might take him home. She lost sight of him again but heedlessly carried on deeper into the wood.

Winded, she stopped to catch her breath. She stood and listened; hoping to hear some sign of him, but the wind was in the canopy above her, whipping branches, and rustling dry leaves all around her. She looked behind her; she could still see the edge of the wood, indicated by a thinness of the trees. She called out to the boy again, but still, there was no reply.

Ellen was torn; she was losing the light as the sun was beginning to set. If she continued, she could become lost herself, though there was a chance she could be there for the child. Or she could turn back now, while she was reasonably certain of getting back to her car, but she would be in effect abandoning the child. She kept thinking, what if he was her child? What must his mother be going through now? Ellen loved children; they were why she had become a teacher. There was no way she could leave this poor boy to fend for himself.

She turned to continue deeper into the darkening wood, searching roughly for the spot she had last glimpsed him, when she felt a sharp pain in the centre of her back, followed by a numbness which spread quickly out to her limbs. Turning awkwardly around, she lost her footing, and fell. Her vision blurred as she looked up to see a large, dark, amorphous shape descend from a thick branch high overhead, to the earth as if floating, it touched the ground, contracting as it seemed to gather itself. Dazedly, she saw it fluidly begin to rise, unfolding distorted segments of itself, each with a pair of jointed limbs, until it towered over her as she lay prone upon the dirt. A stench akin to rotten meat surrounded it. Ellen could hear it hissing, she could hear its rapid clicking, then her vision spun completely, and darkness took her.

***

Harry drove fast, feeling the need to by the urgency in his heart at the setting sun. As he drove he scanned the oncoming traffic, searching the passing cars for her silver Audi A3. He had been driving for ten minutes, when he saw one coming towards him. His heart trip hammered, as for a moment, he thought that all his fears were unfounded, but then he read the registration, and his heart fell.

Where is she?

As the car went past him, he silently swore at the driver, a middle aged man with brown hair and a moustache.

Harry drove on. He took the shortcut that she would have taken, through the back country roads. After a few minutes of frantic acceleration and cornering, he saw her car parked by his side of the road, facing him. He pulled over in front of it, and got out of the car, locking it. The wind had died, but he zipped up his coat against the cold night, then he used the torch to look into her car. He could see her bag, and coat, were still in there, and the keys were still in the ignition.

What could have made her abandon her car like this?

Harry went around the car, opened the door, took Ellen's keys, locked her car, and put the keys in his pocket. His face was grim. He changed the beam's focus to a wide setting, and searched about the ground for signs of her foot prints. The holes Ellen's heels had made in the brown mud were easily followed; the torch pushed back the increasing darkness, illuminating her tracks ahead of him. He followed them through the field, and up to where she had entered the woods. He could see signs of her passing on the wood's floor; her heels had carved furrows through the dirt as if she had been running. He tracked her into the wood, never slowing.

Was she running to or from something?

There were no other prints around. Harry gripped the torch in his big hand, its weight and strength reassuring to him in the darkness. Ahead, he could see that her foot prints had stopped, and that a wide area in the carpet of leaves was disturbed. Harry looked the area over, searching for some sign. From under some fallen leaves the torchlight illuminated something shining white. He stooped to pick it up; it was his wife's school I.D. card that usually hung around her neck; white plastic card, blue plastic frame, purple cord. Ellen's beautiful, smiling face looked up at him from the card. Someone had attacked her. Harry clenched his whole body, hard, against the chill that ran down his spine.

He began to search about for tracks but could find none, when he heard a whimpering, moaning sound, off to his right. Immediately he trained the torchlight on where he gauged the sound to have come from, but the beam was still on wide focus. In amongst the trees about thirty feet away he saw a blue material shape, but that wasn't what drew his attention; the torchlight was playing off what looked like a network of silver threads attached to the top of it, which merged into a thin silvery rope that went up into the canopy. With the beam, he followed it up, and what he saw made him recoil in shock. An inky blackness that the torchlight seemed to slide off, seemed to be perching on a high bough, holding, in what appeared to be a pincer, the length of silvery rope, like a fishing line.

Frozen to the spot, Harry could only look on as the thing hissed at him and swung under the bough, descending via another silvery web rope attached to its base. He could see the creature more clearly now, and it reminded him of a huge spider or ant. On some level he knew, that this creature was responsible for Ellen's disappearance. As soon as its first limbs reached the ground, it ran at him. Something in Harry broke then, his fear turned to rage, and he ran at it howling. Harry swung the torch into its oncoming head with all his force, sending it sprawling. Black slime splattered the floor from a crack in the monstrosities head, its many limbs flailed until it had righted itself. It seemed to look him up and down while it contracted, and then began to rise up to its full height.

The aberration must have stood at least ten feet tall; a low hissing came from it like a warning, its hideous limbs clicking off each other. Suddenly its lower abdomen came forward, and a barb shot out from it at Harry, who twisted sideways narrowly avoiding it. Pressing its advantage it charged Harry, pouncing upon him, and bearing him to the ground.   Harry twisted this way and that, as sharp pincers tried to impale him on either side. It caught him, gouging a burning trench along his left side. He barely noticed. Harry lashed out with the torch, beating about its body; he hit a joint squarely, smashing off one of its appendages. Throwing both arms around it, he used the torch as a bridge for his bear hug; mustering all his rage and force, he crushed the creature's carapace. It screamed and thrashed, knocking Harry's grip loose, then it turned, and ran. Harry roared pure primal rage, and gave chase keeping the torch trained on it. The thing noticeably swayed as it ran; its body dipped in the middle, though it still moved with an alarming rapidity.

The creature was running straight for a cliff wall, but it barrelled through a bush into an unseen cave, followed by Harry. Its cave lair was small, and he saw it was standing over something large, cocooned in the silvery web, hissing as if it were guarding it. Harry looked about, picked up a rock, and threw it at the cocoon; a scream of pain came from it, echoing around the cave, sending the creature into a fit of rage. It moaned and hissed and clicked its limbs, before launching itself at Harry, though Harry was expecting this. He moved deftly to the side and brought his torch down on its head, smashing it to the floor, opening the crack in its head a little wider. He raised his boot, and stamped on its head, again and again, until there was nothing recognisable left but its twitching body and a vile mess on the floor.

Harry knelt by the cocoon, tearing it apart; he had recognised his wife's voice in that cry. Uncovering her at last, he held her in his arms, whispering her name over and over in the dark.

'Harry.'

'Yes, my love.'

'Harry... I love you.'

'I love you too.'

'Harry?'

'Yes dear.'

'Harry please... *kill* me!'

Confused, Harry stepped back and shone his torch on her; she was sweating, and bloated, and bruised all over. Then he saw what he had missed in the darkness; her usually flat stomach was huge and distended, as if she were in her final trimester. He tore open her shirt. The surface of her swollen belly undulated, as though a baby were moving and kicking within. Then she screamed.

Terror gripped him as her body was wracked by sudden violent spasms. He tried to go to her, but he was rooted to the spot. She screamed again, and then fell silent. From under her skirt, between her legs, and from out of her open mouth, tens of the creatures came, each as big as a kitten.

Harry stared in horror as they skittered towards him.

He did not move when they started to climb him.

Harry made no sound as they began to bite him.

A Dream in a Cemetery

Franklin Charles Bishop

Prologue

*If life is but a dream…
then death is the awakening!*

Percy Bysshe Shelley, the great Romantic poet of the early 19th century, had an obsession with death, particularly his own. He called death, "...the final great adventure..." and the thought of drowning as a way into that fearful portal of oblivion appealed to his morbid sensibilities. In fact his dark desire came to pass because he drowned off the coast of Italy in 1822. His fearfully bloated and fish bitten corpse was washed up on the shore of Spezia and cremated under Italian laws on the beach.

Prior to his death just a few days before, Shelley claimed that he had actually seen his doppelganger—an exact image of himself—walking on the balcony of his shoreline villa. Seeing one's doppelganger is a prelude to one's death according to superstition. The old saying, "The good die young," whilst it may not be strictly applicable to Shelley does seem to resonate with his gnawing appetite to hasten to the taste of death.

A one-time associate of Shelley was the Anglo-Italian John William Polidori—an aspiring Romantic poet and novelist. Both were in the intimate confidence of the notorious Lothario and infamous 6th Lord Byron. Whilst with Lord Byron, Polidori wrote a novella entitled, *The Vampyre; A Tale* published in 1819 and which immediately became a best-seller across England and Europe thanks to its seismic change upon traditional English vampire literature. Polidori created the now iconic handsome, amoral and ruthless lady-killer vampire in the form of a wealthy aristocrat—a vampire who was not as portrayed in ancient mythology as an animated rotting corpse risen from the grave to torment members of his former family but instead much more menacing as a man frequenting high society in London, attending grand evening parties and preying upon beautiful ladies of equal rank. A monster who could be the man making idle chatter to your nearest and dearest…

The facts I have related were inspirational in the creation of the story you are about to read and I give them as reference points that you may like to investigate yourself. Although the story is concerned with the Victorian view of death and loss it has links to the early 19th century and also contemporary urban existence with its largely disengagement from the issues of death and oblivion.

Although classed as a work of fiction much of this story is based in truth and recollections of childhood. I confess that there is something of an unquiet presence permeating the following pages that I distinctly felt when writing the tale. What you may feel when reading this testament I can only guess at but others have told me that a tangible odour of decaying English roses effuse the atmosphere no matter where you are. Victorians believed that to smell decaying roses indicated an imminent death nearby—so do have a care about your actual location before commencing to read this tale since I cannot be held responsible for any resulting and unsettling deaths occurring, especially that of your own.

Franklin Charles Bishop
Great Pulteney Street,
City of Westminster, London.

THE CEMETERY

It was one of those extraordinary days that stay forever in the memory. A memory locked in and every time you recall it, as needle sharp as ever in the mind's eye. In absolute clarity with every detail in razor sharp focus—not only visual details but even the smell of freshly placed garlands of sad, weeping roses still haunt my senses with unerring accuracy. Even the gossamer delicacy of the breeze on that day seemed to brush my face as I thought of the memory. The memory was all of thirty years ago, when I was just 9 years of age. My grandFather must have been in his late 60s then.

I had been whispering in my youthful intended respectful innocence to my grandFather as we walked through the large urban cemetery that day. He suddenly turned to look at me saying, "Never whisper in a cemetery!" He said it not harshly but definitely louder than he normally spoke and it made me start in surprise.

I recall asking him if he would show me the city corporation cemetery on Mansfield Road in Nottingham. It was something that as a child I took a naïve view of and I wanted to experience what it would be like to walk among the scary but fascinating Victorian grandiose stone carved figures of angels.

Often whilst sitting in the back seat of my Father's car when he was driving us back home from Nottingham I had glimpsed through the windows the expansive cemetery grounds and gothic funeral statues. But my Father having a total dislike of cemeteries and refusal to discuss death and dying in any shape or form never enlightened me as to why the cemetery was so large and impressive. I wanted to walk in the grounds and see up close the amazing stone carved angels and monolithic structures. There was no chance my Father would ever take me around the cemetery.

My grandFather Harold Hindley was a kindly man and always made a fuss of me so one day he surprised me by telling me that he'd take me for a walk to see the cemetery. It was a nice summery day and he explained prior to setting off that it was known as 'The Rock Cemetery' due to it being built on an outcrop of sandstone rock. I did not know then that it was arguably the city of Nottingham's equivalent to the famous and huge Highgate Cemetery in London. I had no idea that my whim to walk through the Nottingham cemetery would have momentous implications in my future life—had I known then I most certainly would not have ever asked my grandFather or anyone else to take me there on a visit. But childhood is a far distant and ghostly land when viewed from adulthood and it is with incredulity that we visualise our self in a state of innocence in the world. Like looking at an old faded photograph and thinking, "…was that really me?"

But am I in any fundamental way different to the thin, quiet and shy curly haired young boy now that I am grown into a man? Innocence once lost can never be returned or reinstated and that is the tragedy we suffer for being human. Who doesn't look back with regret and remorse?

But I was no philosopher back then and as a result life was much simpler. Being looked after, being loved by grandmother and grandfather, Mother and Father and all the other relatives—looking back, I took it all for granted (what else could I have done?) Like all kindnesses you only truly recognise it when it has gone. I took it as being quite natural for adults to demonstrate to me their kindness. I was a child living in the pleasure principle but now I see it as a miracle, this kindness showered upon me. I didn't realise back then that in this mortal world there were other adults, other children even who did not show kindness but instead showed malevolence. I had no concept of that as a child. That awareness would come later in life.

I looked up at my grandfather and said, "Why? Why can't you whisper in a cemetery…?" Still maintaining his usual very fast walking pace he turned his thin, kindly face to look down at me and said, "Oh, because it's very bad Reuben". He called me affectionately 'Frankie' rather than my proper name of 'Franklin' and I rather liked him because of this. Despite the vast difference in our ages he was to me always distinguished by his mercurial speed of walking. I had to virtually run to keep up with him and whenever he left the house it was essential to watch him speed off down the road until he disappeared out of sight. I inherited some of that speediness of walking in adulthood and have always taken pride in getting from A to B under my own leg power without dawdling. That accounts for my dislike of the ubiquitous urban state-of-the-art shopping mall where the snail's pace of movement by shoppers irritates me greatly even today.

I persisted as much as I dared with my questioning, "Why is it very bad?" —A child's innocent question full of curiosity and longing to be answered. My grandFather now spoke in a much more measured tone to me, Amongst all these graves there are horrible things that you don't want to disturb.' 'What things?' I inanely answered. 'Now I don't want you to be frightened, see…" "I won't be frightened…" I replied without a lot of conviction. My grandfather's response was, "You must never whisper in a cemetery because you'll attract vampires…!"

Now at the age of nine I really knew nothing about vampires or what they were so naturally I hoped that my grandfather would tell me more about them. Of death and all of its formalities in matters of procedures and disposing of bodies I knew nothing. I remember when my grandmother on my Father's side who lived in Bushey Heath near London died I refused to go to the funeral saying, "I don't like funerals!" As a result I was left in the charge of a kind neighbour whilst the rest of the family went to Golder's Green cemetery in London.

In an effort to assuage my questions concerning where to dead people go my Grandfather said:

> Most of them go to Heaven. But some people who have done wicked things in their life, well they of course go to Hell. And sometimes people come back from Hell to haunt the living—but don't you fret about that Frankie my boy because no-one is going to come back and haunt you, or me or anyone else for that matter, see it is only the bad people who come back to haunt other bad people who are still alive.

It was succinctly explained but as a young boy it took me a while to fully understand. And it was quite frightening really. But I remembered his mentioning vampires—what were they I wondered? GrandFather must have read my thoughts because without a word from my mouth he continued speaking:

> Vampires you see, Reuben, are what the bad people who are dead come back to life as. And they—as vampires—come back to haunt others.

'Why mustn't we whisper then?' I queried:

> Cemeteries like this are the resting place for all of the dead people, their bodies only since their souls like I told you have gone to Heaven to be with God. But the bad people don't rest in their graves, no—they become vampires. And in becoming vampires they come out of the graves and appear as they once were alive, but they only show themselves after dark. In daylight they are unable to appear for the sun would burn them instantly to ashes. When visitors come to the cemetery, like us now, if we talk in whispers it attracts the evil vampires because they hear it and think we are whispering because we are afraid of them! So always in a cemetery speak with a normal voice and never be afraid! That way the vampires will never bother you, do you see now, Rueben?

It was a lot for me to understand at the time but I just about had an inkling of what it was all about. The rest of that afternoon was time spent walking through the avenues of stone angels and past huge family mausoleums in high Victorian Egyptian style. The faces of the angels particularly caught my attention—their grief was so intense that I almost thought I saw real tears issuing from the eyes and fancied that they would suddenly come to life and fly off into the sky. I did not like the idea of vampires lurking around and was absolutely determined that I would never visit a cemetery on my own.

20 Years Later

There is a lot to be said for being 30 years old. Family ties are still strong and everyone still makes a fuss over you. The pleasure principle still operates even though you don't realise it. My parents had moved out of industrial Nottingham and we now lived in a commuter belt some twenty-five minutes by car into the city centre. I had already flunked Art College and was working in an incredibly boring engineering office producing technical illustrations for fork-lift truck operating manuals: living only for the weekends and counting the hours and minutes every working day until it was time to go home; bees in a hive, ants in the colony, me in the system. What I had not done however was lose my interest in the morbid. I was fascinated by Gothic literature, Period Gothic that is; Ann Radcliffe, William Beckford and Maturin. I was knee deep in them and reading them all of the time. Desolate castles, spectral monsters appearing in the night, skulls and bones and graveyards were always crowding into my mind.

My interest in the Gothic extended to architecture and in particular the Victorian high Gothic style associated with the houses of that time. Looking back it may have been as a result of my childhood being spent in a late Victorian period house. Tremendously high ceilings in all the rooms, ornate plaster architraves and decorative pillars; the dark, gloomy wooden bannisters on the stairs and the menacing cellar with its precarious very steep steps leading down into the vault-like claustrophobic bare brick cell that served as a receptacle for piles of coal for the open grate fireplaces in each room above. Whilst my earliest infancy found me under the care of my GrandMother and GrandFather on my Father's side (who lived in Bushey Heath near London) from the age of 7 years I was under the care of my GrandMother on my Mother's side who lived in what to me then was an incredibly large and imposing three-storey Victorian period house situated not too far away from the Nottingham City Cemetery.

My GrandMother's house was crowded with heavy, dark wood furniture in every room. The tables were always covered in thick, heavy velvet tablecloths with wonderful tassels. The chairs were as heavy as stone and not for slouching in. The highly decorative though faded wallpaper featured in every room other than the kitchen. The days were long then, or so they appeared to me and the dimly lit interior of the house suited my character. I liked its privacy and sense of isolation from the outside world. Although the cellar frightened me the rest of the house I thought had a friendly atmosphere; it seemed timeless and I believed that my GrandMother had never lived anywhere else.

When my GrandMother died I felt sad that this fine period house would no longer be inhabited by her kind presence. Years later when it was demolished I went back to see an empty space where once my childhood had been enacted. Now all of the vast Victorian villas have been knocked down and the area has been redeveloped and supplanted with hideously industrial boxes called community housing and I cannot even bear to drive past and look upon the scene of my childhood.

My fascination with cemeteries although not obsessive began to take a stronger hold on my life since it linked in seamlessly with my penchant for the Victorian Gothic in architecture. I actively sought out and meticulously planned visits to the Nottingham cemeteries featuring Gothic graves and memorials. But it was still the Mansfield Road City Cemetery that had some strange hold over me or rather my imagination. I took photographs of the marble angels and enlarged them so I could study every nuance of emotion on their faces. The Victorian sentimentality over death held me in thrall. Whereas contemporary society dresses death up antiseptically and distances it from the living the Victorians had an intensity of intimacy with the deceased. They celebrated the death of a loved one in both a glorious public and private display of morbidity involving a multitude of ceremonies and procedures that had to be strictly observed. The Victorians looked death in the face with all of its unbearable horror whilst today we treat it as something to be quickly dismissed and put out of sight.

I began to research Victorian superstitions regarding the death of a family member and how they created memorabilia to honour the memories of their deceased loved ones. I was moved by their attitude to photographs of the dead—literally. Whilst today we would consider having on display a photograph of the corpse of a relative or spouse as definitely a macabre thing to even contemplate the Victorians thought it was the right way to remember the dead. Even dead babies would be photographed, posed to look as though still alive or just sleeping—these photographs would be honoured in a frame and displayed in the parent's bedchamber. Morbid to a modern audience but to the Victorians it was a reminder of the living child and some kind of comfort during the grieving period. Often the photograph would eventually be consigned to a family album after a suitable period had passed but some families would keep the photograph on display permanently.

And thus the study of Victorian funereal traditions and all of its myriad related superstitions became my *raison d'être*. Epitaphics interested me greatly and I became addicted to visiting cemeteries and graveyards featuring high Gothic style, Victorian funerary architecture and memorials. My visits were planned meticulously well in advance as I did not drive or own a car. Pouring over obtuse corporation bus timetables my calculations were almost Pythagorean in nature having to take into consideration the complexities of cemetery opening times and of course the occasional funeral taking place (usually where the Victorian graveyard had been extended in modern times to accommodate the new arrivals so to speak). From planning a week ahead I perfected my timetable reading skills to such a degree that I could plan months in advance my visits to the dark shaded groves of Hades' eternal empire. My greatest pleasure was to wander in complete solitude almost in rapture amongst the graveyards and feel the substantiality of the Victorian wish in a strange sense to keep alive those souls interred beneath grieving angels of stone and marble. I began to undertake meticulous and time consuming research into the occupants couched in eternal sleep beneath memorials that particularly caught my interest. The male Dickensian names of Ebenezer, Julius, Chester, Ira and Rufus and the female names of Beulah, Etta, Estella, Cecelia, Opal and Myrtle carved in timeless and elegant italics conjured up visions of large Victorian families residing in their magnificently grand villas. A distant age, a timeless age where death was honoured by respect and official mourning conformed to set Conventions of behaviour.

As each facet of Victorian funerary behaviour revealed itself to my visits and studies so my obsession deepened even further to the extent that my whole topic of thought throughout every day was concerned with seeking more knowledge of the subject and my deviations into the most obscure of details was compulsive to a marked degree. The inscriptions on the graveyard headstones and monuments sharpened my appetite for tracing from newspaper obituaries the location of the deceased—the cemetery, the graveyard, the site, location and finally actually visiting the site to pay homage almost as a relative to the dead person.

I considered myself not as a mere academic collecting data from grave inscriptions but as a true griever of the particular family whose funeral monument I was viewing. With my whole heart I felt piercing sorrow for dear Beatrice who died in August 1887 the daughter of Silas and Ida. The brief but touchingly tender inscription which read:

Sweet flower, transplanted to a clime where never comes the blight of time

I discovered other inscriptions that made me shiver and reduced me to tears with their declared defiance that the grave did not truly hold their loved one and that the spirit had flown elsewhere to dwell forever in a higher realm:

I know his face is hid under the coffin lid, Closed are his eyes, Cold is his forehead fair,
My hand that marble felt, O'er it in prayer I knelt, Yet my heart whispers that He is not there

Thus were my seasons passed, each finding me travelling to distant cemeteries, graveyards with grandiose but crumbling mausoleums sited on unbearably sad Cyprus lined avenues. The more I researched and found the more knowledge that I longed to seek. Nothing it seemed could quench my thirst for Victoriana graveyard related miscellany. Each enquiry never satisfied but led on to more enquiry and thus off into every more ambiguous and complex observations. You may ask was I aware of my by now increasingly obsessional behaviour? You may as well ask a drunken man if he is aware of his being drunk—he is only aware of the present and if he is drunk then he has arrived—the journey to that condition is of no important or interest to him. So I liken this to myself. To partake of a draught of the world of Victorian bereavement with all of its accoutrements is as heady as drinking absinthe and thus it takes you down into the underworld of the dead.

The Revelation

On reaching the age of 40 something happened to me. All I can do is relate the event and the time leading up to it. They do say confession is the beginning of closure. I suppose that the Victorian mode of dress for funerals may have triggered my descent into a troublesome state—I will let you decide upon that when acquainted with the facts of the case.

Blame the Romans for the Victorian fixation with wearing black for funerals. The Romans believed that wearing black clothing prevented the mourners from being haunted by the ghost of the deceased. The Victorians also took to developing this style into jewellery by wearing Jet—a black/amber mineral. I visited museums with displays of Victorian ladies dresses complete with black crepe for the veil and mourning handkerchiefs made from cambric. I found the keepsakes of hair from the deceased encased in a locket heartbreakingly sad. By wearing black it was believed that the living were invisible to the dead. I concluded that the Victorians were the last society to in effect celebrate death just as the ancient Egyptians had. I compared the clinically and fast cremation much favoured today with the lingering, softly departing of the deceased by the Victorians. The pain is arguably lengthened by the Victorian etiquette of death but surely grieving time allows for an acceptance of the cataclysmic event.

It happened during the winter month of October, a suitably Gothic month in fact. I was making my way to the exit of the Nottingham City cemetery on Mansfield Road at a brisk pace since I had almost forgotten that closing time was minutes away. I was transcribing a long tribute below a sorrowing but imposing marble angel on the far side from the gate entrance. I knew the crusty council worker was a 'job's worth' for shutting on time but I was able enough to climb over the iron railings should I become locked in. In all my visits over the years to the cemetery I had never actually been locked in. To be quite honest I thought "To Hell with it!" A simple phrase but on reflection a very powerful thing to even think of—and I then actually whispered it with some vehemence. Almost at once I knew I had done something that would have terrible consequences. In my mind I heard the ghostly echo of my GrandFather's voice saying, "Never whisper in a cemetery…!" The voice was audible like he had been standing just behind me. In fact I instinctively turned around expecting to see him quite illogically standing behind me! There was no one behind me. But there was all at once a sensation of movement like dancing shadows among some distant monumental angels. In all of my years of cemetery and graveyard exploration I had never felt unease when in a necropolis—sadness, yes even tearful on rare occasions but fear, never.

In my infant years I had vivid memories of sitting in my GrandMother's back room in the Victorian villa and seeing the whole room as though viewed through the wrong end of a telescope. Everything in the room seemed to be far, far away and I became smaller somehow. It was a weird sensation which I never mentioned to anyone throughout my life yet the image remained firmly in my thoughts. It was disturbing because it distorted reality. Now the cemetery was receding away from me in the same manner and I was powerless to stop this odd sensation. Then I realised there was absolute silence in the cemetery. Usually the traffic roar from the parallel main road was ever present but not obtrusive yet now utter silence. Even the grey cloudy sky seemed to be pushing down and restricting me, tightening my breathing, oppressing me physically.

Amongst this silence I began to hear muffled whispering—unintelligible but insistent whispering of a malevolent nature. The kind of whispering you hear behind your back. Not pleasant. There was no one else except me in the cemetery yet the irritating and irritated whispering continued not getting any louder but encircling me and just like the lowering sky seemingly restricting any movement I wanted to make. The cycophagustian angels now appeared larger and loomed over me—their expressions of sorrow had not changed but seemed to be more intense and imbued with life. The intensity of their sorrow was overwhelming me and I felt that I could not bear the full force of their concentration.

My visual and audio senses were on overload and physically I was immobile almost encased in some kind of invisible deep heavy water. Drowning. Then my olfactory senses became flooded with the smell of decaying roses; intense, sickly sweet and stifling every other sensation—then with a juddering jolt—complete stygian blackness. Silence. Oblivion. This then, finally was death? No pain, no sense of physicality. Only the faint odour of decaying roses…

Envoi

The body of Reuben Talman was found quite lifeless in the cemetery by the warden who upon opening the main gates and during his usual inspection of the walkways and graves saw the above named gentleman prostrate at the base of a large memorial angel. There were no signs of a struggle and the face of the deceased was not contorted and indeed showed a quite benevolent visage. Scattered around the deceased were a small number of rose petals in a decayed state although they gave off a surprisingly pleasant sweet odour.

> Dear heavenly one,
> Thou canst not die,
> Mine, mine forever,
> Ever mine.

RETURNING

JOHN STRACHAN

If the dead and the living
  Could talk one to one
Do you think they'd be happy,
  That they'd have lots of fun?

If you could dance with your Father
  Or talk with your mum?
Would you welcome the converse
  Or would you keep schtum?

You could see your old teacher
  From when you were a child.
But what if his features
  That once were so mild

Were haggard and ashen
  And staring and wild?
And your friend from your schooldays,
  Well, would he feel defiled

To be back in this world
  Where he died in a car?
And that child of six months
  Who was 'crossing the bar'?

Would he like to return
  To this world as it is?
The place that he once left,
  Which lacked happiness?

People go when they are ready,
  People go when it's right.
It's not to the dark side,
  It's not to the light.

It isn't to Heaven,
  And it isn't to Hell.
It isn't unwelcome
  And you don't hear a bell.

They don't want to come back.
  That is not what they feel.
That is only our selfishness
  As we still turn the wheel.

The Promised Bride

Janet Cooper

I jerked as the carriage came to a halt. The black door, encased in iron creaked as it opened. In an effort to compose myself, I took a deep breath and slowly leaned my head out of the carriage. The night sky hid my surroundings from me as the strange carriage driver took my hand gently and helped me down each of the wooden steps carefully. His long cloak covered his whole body and did a good job of disguising his curved, hunched spine and his cold, wrinkly fingers. He stared at me in the eye for a few seconds displaying every wrinkle of his old haggard face; his eyes green, wide and wild as if he was a very tortured man.
"Just follow the path until you get to the stone wall" he coughed.
"Trace the wall to the left and you will find the door to the castle".
I stared at him as he unloaded my small suitcase and handed it to me. I looked along the dark path that sloped down into a deep valley and then quickly looked back at the coach driver now mounting the carriage.
"You're leaving me here" I gulped.
He looked at me momentarily, shook the reins and started along the dark road without response.
I put on my shawl and dragged my suitcase along the path, slipping further into the dark wilderness.

I was going to meet the man I would marry, as promised by my ancestors. I had waited for this for a long time, dreaming of being whisked off by a handsome stranger who I would love instantly just as Mother had promised. The trees made taller by their thick, twisted branches cast shadows which followed me through the thick guarded wood. The smell of river weed and stagnant water was lingering in the air; the taste attacking my throat with every breath. I knew that one misjudged footstep could take me down the river bank and into the raging water so I hesitantly traced my path by shuffling my feet.

I quivered as the wind picked up; swaying and twisting the trees, making them cavort around me. The rustling noises behind me and deep whistling sound to my sides, suggested I pick up my pace and canter.
Finally I arrived at a stone wall which was so high it was impossible to see the top. I felt the rough stone and followed it to my left, as the carriage driver had instructed. The wall scraped at my delicate skin bringing spots of blood to the surface.

I didn't bother knocking at the huge door but grabbed the freezing bronze handle, twisting it open dragging my case in with me. Though the hallway was lit with candles, the black marble tiled walls cast an uneasy darkness; their sheen distorting my reflection as I stalked the corridor. I felt sick and almost turned back, but I was here now and curious to meet my husband; embrace my fate.

The stairs at the end of the corridor, led me down. I felt that I was entering the depths of hell itself as nowhere on earth could be this deep. The spiral stairs were steep and got increasingly narrow until they were smaller than my foot which I was now twisting sideways to prevent slipping. As I reached the bottom puffs of ancient dust expelled from the carpet in an attempt to suffocate me.

The corridor opened up into a candle-lit hallway large enough to be a ballroom in itself. Of the many doors only one was open.

I stumbled wearily through the opening as I was exceedingly tired and needed to rest. A roaring fire beckoned me to a chaise longue which I greeted like a long lost friend. A side table offered a steaming pot of tea which I gratefully took advantage of despite a feeling of trepidation as to who might have prepared it. I slouched in a trance for a moment before eventually focussing on the room.

I sat up a little looking at a portrait above the fireplace. I moved slowly from portrait to portrait. The face was identical though the man's attire suggested different eras. The most recent seemed to be of the man side by side with our current Queen, Victoria, but others dated back several centuries; always the same face; a small mole just to the left of his chin.

I was no longer alone; I turned in a start. There he was, the man in the portrait; right beside me. He smiled kindly. His face was white; his lips pale pink. He was well composed; dark suit with jet black hair combed back. He was pouring tea into a cup which he offered to me.

"I'm Claude, and I have been waiting for you" he smiled taking my hand and kissing it gently. His voice was strong, manly, yet soothing.

"Have you noticed the portraits?" he asked

I nodded, sipping the cup.

"You look exactly like your ancestors" I whispered.

He laughed: "My poor naive child, they are all me, not my ancestors".

I knew inside that all was not quite right yet strangely I didn't feel afraid. Claude was so charming.

"I suppose you want to know the secret to my immortality" He said blithely.

I didn't say or do anything; shivers surfing my spine.

I am Immortalis Homo-Aranea

> You are the said one, Eve. It is prophesised in the ancient Aranea scrolls. You can carry my children. Only one born every thousand years can carry Aranea children.

I looked at him and forced a smile. I don't know if I was supposed to appear grateful or faint like a lady. I did neither
"Aren't you excited Eve?"
I nodded. For once in my life I felt significant, important yet in the back of my mind I knew that something was terribly wrong..
Claude leapt to his feet:
'I don't think your excited enough Eve' he snarled, ripping off his shirt and exposing the black mat on his chest. I stared at him, was this man insane?
I watched him carefully as black, spindly legs sprung out of his back and grew larger than he was. They pushed up his body so that he was face down and he twisted and turned his neck until huge teeth burst from his mouth. The giant human spider lowered his face towards me.
Unbelievably I reached up and stroked his face, the same kind face that appeared on the portraits. He calmed down.
"Do my family know what you are?" I asked
"Of course" he said shrinking back to his original size.
"Are you afraid?" he asked, stroking my face.
I shook my head. I wasn't afraid, for the first time I actually felt comfortable, this man had been honest from the moment I entered his home, which is more than I could say for my own family as they failed to mention a lot of important details. I was told that I was promised to a rich, kind, handsome stranger, belonging to a wealthy family.
"I will treat you well Eve, I will look after you. I want to be normal and have a family."
We ate together that evening and Claude explained more about the Arenea species, how they ate humans and kept the lifeless bodies fresh by wrapping them in their web. He promised me a life of riches, promised I would have maids, a nanny and the best nurses and doctors to tend the birth of our children. I was seduced by his promises, his riches and his honesty. All I had to do was bear his offspring.
 Claude held me "Eve" he said, lowering his eyes to the floor "If you don't want to, I understand, you may leave if you wish, but I would love you to become my wife". His voice was so gentle; his eyes told me he was lonely, and would genuinely look after me. I nodded in agreement. I was ready to honour my family's agreement and become his wife, and Mother to his Arenea babies. Even his human feastings did not deter me; in fact, I encouraged them and even brought home a few victims myself.
I rode in golden carriages, dressed in the best silks, wore gloves and attended soirées with my husband. I had a stunning wedding and six months later I became pregnant. As

Claude had promised, I had the best nurses, doctors, the best maids. Everything was perfect and my husband was most loving and supportive.

As I got to the end of the pregnancy I started to become incredibly uncomfortable; the babies kicking eight legs at once. I stayed indoors and my husband told anyone who asked, that I was ill. I was not fazed in the slightest at the thought of my babies eating human flesh; in fact it started to excite me in a horrible kind of way.

The birth was excruciatingly painful; four babies taken away from me immediately they appeared. I was so exhausted; I could not keep my eyes open. I heard my husband at one point but I could not seem to regain consciousness. I kept hearing talking and becoming semi-conscious but I could not distinguish reality from dreams.

I wasn't sure how much time passed but I woke alone. The room was unfamiliar to me; dark and dusty with red symbols painted on floor and ceiling. A font stood prominently in the centre of the room surrounded by a circle of candles. The blood stains on my nightdress looked dry and distorted.

"Hello" I shouted to no avail. I tried to move only to find that I was bound to a huge circular, wooden object.

"You're awake" I heard my husband say.

"Yes. Claude! What's going on? How long was I asleep" I asked politely. This was the first time I had ever felt uncomfortable in Claude's presence.

"It's OK Eve. Though it has been four days" He smiled coyly.

We just need to complete the ancient Aranea ritual, for the boys to be healthy."

"All boys then... are they OK?" I asked.

"They are very healthy, all three of them, we should be very proud".

'Three? But I had four children.' I queried.

"Yes but one was a girl, I dealt with that one" he snarled, curling his lip in disgust.

Something had changed in Claude's voice that made me feel uneasy. He was cold, distant, and certainly not the husband I had come to love over the past year.

Suddenly I was hoisted into the air by the circular object, turned upright, and thrust into the middle of the room close to the font.

I was confused, what had happened to my daughter?

"I don't know what's happening" I said, pleading to Claude for some insight.

"Aranea are only males, females are useless, weak and unable to transform. We always sacrifice our females" he yelled.

"As for you... you have served your purpose!"

"What? Where are my sons? What's going on Claude?" I cried. Panic spread through my body.

"Come out boys" Claude shouted so loudly that it echoed through the wooden room.

Three, black figures crept in from the darkness. They were knee length in height, with eight legs each and they were horrible hissing sounds. They crawled towards Claude's voice and stopped beside him.

"They are not my boys!" I whimpered, looking at three black spiders.

"You are right" Claude grinned, applauding.

"They are not your boys. You were merely an incubator. The eggs are mine and are fertilised inside me before being planted into your body"!

"Have I not been good to you Eve?" he enquired sarcastically.

"'The thing about Aranea, Dear, is that the boys are only able to transform once the ritual has been performed; think of it like a christening." Claude grinned horribly.

    The contents of the font shimmered in the candle-light; a black, viscous substance. Claude's children slowly circled the font. Dipping his feathered black hand into the liquid he inscribed a strange symbol on their disgusting bulbous heads. He started chanting words I had never heard before; I was becoming frantic now.

Claude looked at me with his wild eyes. He gently stroked my face.

"The young must now eat their Mother to be able to fully transform"

I started to scream yet I knew that this was self inflicted. I had been given the chance to leave when I first arrived but I hadn't. I had been bought, like a prostitute.

"Come forth children" Claude commanded.

I stopped screaming and stared in shock as my Mother and little sister appeared. Claude marked my sister's forehead with blood too and began speaking more words I did not understand. He gave her the blood to drink and she took it willingly.

"Don't do it Mary" I yelled, but my fifteen year old sister drank and then left the room, guided by my Mother. This was my penance, I had been the happiest I had ever been, spending Claude's money, having the best of everything and I had allowed my husband's evil to continue, to ensure my petty comforts.

"Your sister's ancestors will produce women for my three sons in another thousand years as I have now blessed her" Claude spat at me as a huge point grew from his head.

"I will make this as painless as possible" Claude whispered to me, injecting me with his venom, paralysing me.

"Feast!" he yelled to the boys and they did not need telling again. They pounced, hissing and snarling, tearing shreds of skin from my body and despite the pain all I could think of was how thirsty I was. "Water" I screamed "Please I need water..."

"They very rarely survive a bite from this spider, Father but I think this one might just make it."

"I do hope so" said the priest "she looks like she's been through the tortures of the damned. I have anointed her with the oil of chrism and given her the Sacrament of the Sick. All we can do now is wait and hope!"

THE VICTIM

GLENN UPSALL

As soon as she walked in she felt the tension. It hit her like her husband's fist. She often didn't see that coming either. He was sitting in the dark, in his favourite chair. The glow of his cigarette giving him away.
"Is there anything you regret?" His voice was soft, yet just as menacing.
She dropped her bag on the sofa, letting out a sigh. *Here we go again....* "Yes." She readied herself for the inevitable explosion. "But you already know that."

***

The Detective sat in his car. He hated his job. Mopping up people's messes, witnessing their trails of destruction. How could people who loved each other, hurt each other so much?
      He looked out at the flashing blue lights, the cordoned-off house, and the crime scene officers in their paper 'onesies'. What was it this time....? Jealous husband? Cheating wife? Homicidal child? Killer cat? He'd seen it all. And to be honest, he'd seen enough.

***

He didn't flinch. Didn't say a word. And in a way, that was worse. He took a long drag on his cigarette. She could feel his eyes burrowing into her. Searching her mind. Scrutinising her body language. Looking for every tell tale sign or nervous tick. Even in the poor light, she could sense he knew she was blushing. Her heart rate had increased, her cheeks flushed red, due to the sudden release of adrenalin into her system.
      This was truly a fight-or-flight moment if ever there was one. She chose flight. She spun on her heels, and made a grab for the door. He was on her before she even made it out of the room. He grabbed her long black hair, wrapping it around his fingers, before yanking her back into the room. He threw her to the floor, and slammed the door. Her hair was tangled between his fingers, bloodied at the roots.
"Please, don't." She pleaded, whilst subconsciously wishing she'd cut her hair short like she'd planned to do. "I love you."
"You don't know what love is!" He screamed at her.
"Look at you....Parading yourself around like a cheap whore while I'm at work 'till all hours!"
"Richard, I swear, I'd never"
Her sentence was cut short as his fist smashed into her cheek. She crumpled to the floor. Her head was spinning. No matter how many times she'd been hit, she never got used to the nauseating dizziness. He dragged her off the floor by her hair.

Damn this hair, so easy to get hold of...

The punch to her stomach doubled her up; winding her. She cried out in pain, unsteady on her heels. He always followed up the head shot with the body blow....she didn't mind, she never had to explain away the hidden bruises. His hands gripped her throat.

This was new...

He squeezed... and squeezed... and squeezed. She looked into his eyes. She'd never seen him like this. His entire face was a mask of hatred. She could feel her windpipe being crushed. Her eyes bulging. The blackness was coming for her, and she welcomed it.

***

The Detective climbed out of his car. The night air whipped at his face, forcing him to pull his collar up around his cheeks. He wished he could be home in the arms of his beautiful wife; holding her close. The smell of her perfume filling his nostrils, as she forced him to watch the latest implausible drama, being played out on one of her numerous soap operas.
He would tease her. Explaining how these streets had a higher body count over the years than any horror movie he knew of.

If only she knew what real death looked like... she wouldn't be so keen to watch then, would she?

***

The blackness almost had her. The life was being squeezed out of her. It's true what they say, your life does flash before your eyes. And what she saw didn't impress her. What had she actually achieved? Mediocre exam results, a pointless Open University Degree, a dead end job, an abusive husband, and a vicious pet cat.
I'm worth better than this...
She clawed at his face, digging her nails into his skin. He yelped. The first time she'd ever heard him show signs of weakness. He was forced to release her. The breath poured into her lungs.

Oh my God, she could hurt him...

She pushed him off her. He wasn't this unbeatable monster. This terrifying enigma. He was just a man.
She smiled to herself. She would leave him. Build a new life. A life she could be proud of. She was stronger than him mentally and at this exact moment, physically. For the first time in her life she was content. The future belonged to her. He smashed her head

against the corner of the coffee table shattering her temple. Bone fragments pierced her brain, killing her instantly, like a bullet from a gun. She lay motionless on the deep pile rug, as the blood ran down her face. She was still smiling.

***

 The Detective nodded at the Uniform standing sentry at the door, and stepped into the house. He looked at the smiling couple staring back at him from the picture frame in the hallway.

Bet they're not smiling now...

He was greeted by his Sergeant at the scene.
"It's not pretty in there-" He stopped. "Hey, what happened to your face?"
Detective Tanner touched the scabbed scratches on his cheek.
"Bloody cat. It'll be the death of me one of these days."
The Detective looked at the blonde handcuffed woman sitting at the kitchen table. Her blood-soaked husband lying on the floor, knife protruding from his ribcage. Her bruised face looked up at him with mascara streaked eyes. They shone with life. Finally.

Welcome to the Hell Hole

Lindsay Bingham

I know from the moment I walk into the bar I am looking for trouble. My heels clack on the crooked old floorboards announcing my entrance to the phlegmatic old timer behind the bar. He doesn't even give me the eye or the once over as he knows his gold tooth is the only thing he owns worth a damn. Hell even the rims on my ride are worth more and that's parked out front, like I couldn't give a crap. This guy's merely a shadow in the moonglade cast across the countertop. He's reflected in the blemish from years of spilled hops rubbed clear by some good old fashioned elbow grease. He knows every inch of that counter better than the back of his hand; his skin is heavily scarred and hardened from an old crow's age of desert sun and stepping in on too many bar fights. The worst scar I can make out runs from his cheek through his brow and snakes off under his eye. Dressed in a bull horn necklace, jeans and a black tee he looks as happy to be here as the old bear head mounted on the wall. The bar can only be described as a hole, ready at the edge of the desert waiting for the earth to open up and swallow it whole. Funnily enough the name above the door roughly translates to 'The Hell Hole'. I guess I came to the right place then.

With miles and miles of nothing but darkness and a dog day moon, this shithole is a very welcome eyesore. Not that the old man ever rolls out the red carpet or nothing. My cheeks sting from the day's inescapable sun and the restless heat boils my blood still. Even though the day is over, the inferno is inescapable and constant. Its sweaty barrage means it's too hot for leathers but I wear mine because the jacket goes damn fine with the boots. Those vexing clacks on the bare wood as I make my way to the bar draw little attention to the bad mood that consumes me. I can feel the rain oozing off my hair and down my clothes soaking the floor in my wake. The smell of the desert sand dries my throat making me need sustenance. Not a frosty pitcher or an iced cold draft but something far grittier on the soul. It's not like I even have to ask for a drink before one's thrust under my nose. The barman wise and experienced can decipher the desired tipple of a man from ten paces; I'd suspect that it is written all over my face if I didn't wander in from time to time, always drinking the same, two chasers and a one for the road. I guess it is the same with the four other men in the bar; the two knuckleheads slouched at the end of the counter keeping their conversation to themselves and the lonesome, heartbroken man seeking consolation from the jukebox. He's the only one that even lifts his head to acknowledge my presence, the hooch making him daring. They're as hopeless as me; except they make it their place to come in here every night hoping that tonight's the night when one of them is going to get lucky. Not that they ever will. I just want a hard drink and I think after the day I've had I deserve it. Not wanting to go into detail but it involves a clumsy oaf, a carelessly parked car, my foot and his face.

It's close to the witching hour and the temperature shows no sign of dropping, the stagnant smell of tobacco, sweat and stale beer bewitches my senses. The lull from some oldie on the jukebox disrupts the silence between the three strangers who have nothing to talk about; the two at the end of the bar are faring little better. Having grown up together futile conversations have become somewhat of a second nature to them. They talk about drink, cars and women. There is little else in their humdrum lives to talk about. Not that there are a lot of women around these parts, believe me I've looked. They blow into town one day like a warm summer breeze and blow on out again once they've seen the sights. It normally takes at least an hour, tops. That's why the old timer behind the bar called this place 'The Hell Hole', with the incessant heat, the lack of women and the stimulating conversations.

I can't think of a worse fate than living here. It's the kind of place where everyone knows everyone else's business, which is why I keep myself to myself. I'm just the stranger, who lives on the edge of town, it's been like this for years and I want it to remain that way. With the four stools at the bar and the knuckleheads taking up all but two of them, the guy at the jukebox filling up the view of the window that leaves only one of the table seats. The half-a-sleep trucker's curled up round his pitcher on a table between jukebox Joe and the bar. He's drooling all down his chin and over the table top but he's none the wiser. I take my usual seat. As far in the corner as I can get from the hairy bar huggers and Sleeping Beauty. The grinding of wood against wood as I slide out my chair slices through the bar like a freight train through a wall. I'd apologise for being so loud if I gave a shit.

Lugging my snifters over to the table I set them down in a way that any sulking man would. The resounding thud of the glasses and the way their rims clink together already starting to make me feel more sociable; as sociable as I like to get anyway. The seats warped and it groans under my weight. Once it's settled no one's going to even notice my presence till I'm gone. The first sip works hard and fast, every bit the deadly poison it's meant to be. The glass and its contents are hotter than a whore house on nickel night; the numbing after burn of the poison satisfying in the way only whiskey can be. Sips of the second chaser fully numb my throat as the rest of the world evaporates.

I'm rudely interrupted when thunder jolts the old tin roof. The drumming of rain thrashing the roof drowns out Jukebox Joe's drunken limericks to his half-forgotten love songs. The barflies finally stop yammering to take in the sound of the rain, though it hasn't distracted the old timer from shining up his reflection on the bar top some more. I return my glass not quite to my lips to take in my third sip when trouble rolls on in.

The sweet smell of fear and lady sweat blows in to the bar like an aphrodisiac and it smells a whole lot like fresh cherries. She shivers from her head to toe, ringing out her wet locks by the door as she's brought the rain in with her. The raindrops roll down her naked thighs as if they are too firm and supple to settle there. Clad in nothing but a pair of cut off denims and black vest the rain caught her by surprise, as she does every warm blooded male in the place. She has found the only bar in town and from the rise and fall of her chest she looks flustered. She's either walked far or fears the thunder. Could she have been running to escape the rain or is her story filled with woe and some violent Romeo?

She creeps up to the bar like some fretful alley cat. The old timer hands her the crusty rag that he keeps under the counter. Never one to extend the same reception to any other of his patrons, she should consider this his special treatment. Though I can't blame him I can just about taste the salty goodness of the rain and sweat rolling its way down between her breasts, along her clavicles and down those juicy thighs. She's the new stranger in town and because of the junk hidden between her legs everyone treats her differently; it's in the stares of those barflies drooling on the bar. Jukebox Joe has changed his tune and the old timer stands patiently waiting on her every word. Sleeping Beauty and me are the only ones in the room who can about keep our tongues in our mouths, but he's still snoring so it doesn't count. I act cool and pretend not to notice her. The only ice cool thing in the bar is my expression and she doesn't even bother to notice it.

She leans over to ask for a drink from the old timer and I can't quite catch what she's ordered as I'm too busy eavesdropping on the barflies' intentions. They've started smiling and casually slithering along the counter leaving a seat between them for her to take. Cleverly she keeps the conversation to a minimum with the two delinquents. Drying her hair with one hand she leaves the bar and scouts out the rest of the seats. The two overconfident dicks take to following her with their eyes till she decides on the table next to mine. Maybe it was the six feet tall silent leather toting stranger taking up the corner or the thought of having nothing worthy to offer this girl; they swivel back around in their chairs and hang their heads in shame. The one piece of ass that blows into town and they missed their chance. I can't help but hide the smirk from the corners of my mouth, but I just keep my head down and sip my drink.

She sits with her back to the wall taking in the bar. Just sitting there like a fruit basket full of ripe and juicy fruit, dabbing at the beads of sweaty rain rolling down her skin, barely even contemplating her effect on the disheartened barflies. The journey back to their stools was far too great a walk of shame for them to handle; they had miles to go yet before the liquor would made them numb enough to cope with such a hard knock like a rejection from her. They still eye her every move wildly like a hungry dog eyeing a juicy chicken thigh.

Towelling the wet out of her wild dark locks she too does her share of eyeing up, hers instead fixed on the door. Even as she runs her fingers through her roots she's jumpy. The door groans and the wind howls outside. Her eyes instinctively trained on the one and only door like she's ready to make her escape. I hate to admit it but mine too are busy, taking in every inch of her curves, the whole fruit basket; those ample melons, that peachy ass, those plum lips, and her pear shaped hips. She is certainly a delight to behold there is no denying that. With skin the colour of the sand in a blood red desert she could have easily gotten that from long days of walking the road, or even outback behind the bar.

Though her spaghetti heels are not the kind of thing meant for walking the open road, judging from the dirt and sand on her heels she's done her fair share of haunting the highway. Her face, I can't see but she looks nervous and scared. She settles in the chair close to me, just out of arm's reach but close enough for me to listen to the rise and fall of her chest.

Her presence is somewhat soothing to me; it brings a gentle solace to my mood like watching a sun set or listening to the ocean. I swear I can hear her heart beat its rhythm out of time with mine.

Waiting for the storm to pass little Cherry is forced to take in the highlights of a rundown old mining town. A few shacks and a seedy motel mark the edge of town; roads and plenty of them all leading nowhere. Sand and tumbleweeds, a rundown garage and an old store, there is nothing more.

The views are the only thing going for this place; by day miles and miles of rugged unspoiled terrain, but by night all is veiled in darkness. Once you hit the highway there is always more reason to go than stay but I always find some reason to return.

She herself must have got turned around somewhere to find herself in this dive; lost which road is the one that led out of town. Silently, I'm brooding over how crazy the brunette's making me feel; my palms are sweaty and my clot-catcher pounding in my chest like a junkie going into withdrawal. I'm normally one for solitude but her sitting there, all so close to me is turning my whiskey sour. The sugary slow time I'm taking in sipping them down is tempering my chasers to that of such a sticky night. I'm still as the wind on a warm summer's day quietly enjoying the company without her even knowing it. The seconds turn into minutes and the minutes turn into a lifetime. She could sit there forever and I won't mind; hell I won't even notice the ravaging sands of time slip away the youth from my bones. Does she even know I'm there? I hold my breath as she awkwardly scans the room again. Perhaps she won't even notice me, if I keep still long enough...

Whatever she's drinking its cold and the bubbles slowly meander their way up to the rim of her glass. The glass itself is sweating. Ringing the table every time she drinks; downing the last of it in a few gulps she's in no hurry to stay or she's grown too wary of all of us complete and utter losers. I still act like I haven't noticed her as she gets up to leave. Not that she's paid me in kind. My eyes lusting after her as she stands and makes her way back over to the bar; she may as well have ripped out my heart and taken it with her.

Thanking the barman for the drink, she pays and heads to the leaker with the crusty bar towel in her hand. That's why I swiftly down the rest of my second chaser pissed at myself for not having the gall to even crack a smile in her direction. She hasn't so much as noticed me; me being there not doing anything except pussyfooting around. She lives in the now and I still live in the then; going over every detail of her in my mind.

The sound of a failing engine roars through the bar and I don't pay it much attention or the several sounds of grit crunching underfoot. Cherry is too lovely to mess in the night with a dark creature like me.

She's in the rest room for what seems like an eternity when in from the road blows a whole new world of mayhem.

Three losers, riddled and infested with bad guy syndrome, walk in to the bar. One having mastered the walk he thinks belongs to a modern day cowboy. He's about five ten and as ugly as a hat full of assholes.

Another of his crew, all pretty, like a hairless-monkey selfishly digs out an oversized handful of nuts from the dish on the counter carelessly spilling the rest over the old timer's well-polished countertop.

The other, a true un-gentleman clad in denim, elbows one of the barflies in the back both purposely and skilfully, like he's done it before. The fellow chokes on his pint and Denim doesn't offer to buy him a new round; what a dick!

From the bar flies' restrained reactions they recognise the three unwise men; piping down, drinking up and scarpering on into the night.

The new patrons just cut deep into the old timer's nightly profits and the old man knows it all too well. He scowls adding ten years on to his leathered face.

I don't need this... I just came in for a drink or three. I can hear the irritating scrape of chairs close to Sleeping Beauty and the clatter of him hitting the floor after Denim kicks his chair out from under him.

Like a gaggle of geese I want to strangle the life out of, they mock Sleeping Beauty's ever so rude awakening. They've taken to sharing about his booze. Taking turns in swallowing from the ice cool pitcher they spare no thought to the bloodied and shitfaced drunk sprawled out like a new animal skinned addition to the bar floor. He grumbles something considerably pathetic, even for a drunk before he passes out. Their presence irks me into focusing on the feeling at the bottom of my next glass. A few more sips and I'm leaving, throwing back the firewater because I can't stand to be there with those fools hanging around.

It's written all over the old timer's face: he wants them there as much as I do.

I start to grind my teeth, ignoring the bad smell taking over the room.

Jukebox Joe keeps to himself, which is rather pitiful for a round man in his fifties. Though until they walked in he was humming and singing what words he could remember of songs he vaguely remembered now he just hugs that music machine like his life depends on it.

The hairless monkey clambers up and laughs in Joe's face, using up the last of his credits selecting anything but Joe's country and love songs. The juke box turns over some racket that the ape selected. Heavy metal fuelled by teenage angst, intolerable screaming, an assault on the eardrums.

Denim polishes off the dregs in Sleeping Beauty's pitcher before he hurls it across to the wall behind old timer at which point Cherry rushes back into the room, apprehensively biting on her delicious lip. Her timing couldn't have been any unluckier; they're as surprised to see her as she is them. Her timing is no good at all.

Hairless monkey slithers up from behind her ready to claim his prize by force. Denim man stands up not so much asking her to join him as telling her.

The finger-pointing has started, waved in her face like a poisoned carrot offered to an unruly mare. I can just imagine how easily it would crush under my grip; the mental image does little to animate my facial features they're set to their usual dour, brooding pose.

The resounding crunch still lingering in my ears, I so want to bend it until Denim points back at himself. I focus on my drink again, casually taking in the action by the bar, just like I don't give a crap. She shakes her head but finds the word 'no' stuck in her throat, like most scared broads. Hairless monkey drags her by the damp roots convincing her otherwise. Cowboy by the bar laughs as he too throws back some nuts. He doesn't care that he spilled half of them on old timer's floor. Denim the prettiest of the three morons nervously runs his hands through his hair engaging in idle chitchat with Cherry as he pressures her into taking the seat next to him. His eyes as eager to rough the little lady up as his hands are, he starts openly stroking her neck from which she shies away too politely. He then runs his hand up her arm and I can sense her tensing up. Lowering my head as though I'm not interested in what's going on I look to the old timer who's more frustrated than he is capable of playing the hero. The scene is making the hard lines on his face intensify. I suspect he's sick of them tearing up the joint at every opportunity, they all forget it's still his bar.

Hairless monkey cranes his neck to scan around the room; he's looking for trouble but not the kind I'm packing. He does a double take pretending he doesn't see me but he clocks me sitting all the same. I do him the courtesy of making out that I don't notice him notice me. My presence causes him alarm as he doesn't know what to make of me. I'm just the loner sitting at the back of the bar; a shadow in a mere shithole, in a small corner of the world. Denim is still getting all handsy with Cherry, smearing the fresh sweet smell of cherries all over his grubby hands. His thumb rubs off the carefully applied lip gloss from her mouth. He visibly relishes the sweet taste left on his thumb. That's another appendage of his I want to break. It's as good as kissing her and he knows it. Forcing her to look at him, he's hurting the little Miss and despite her protests he's unrelenting. She's already reaching for Sleeping Beauty's discarded glass, thrashing it into her would be kisser's face. Denim, instantly appalled and enraged, slaps the little hell-raiser across the cheek till she's on the ground. The two other grease-monkeys are at the bar hooting as we all know what's coming; he drives in a few kicks for good measure. A real man such as he can't handle any woman's rejection, especially since his friends are around to see it. There's a lesson going to be learned and dipshit Denim wants to be the one teaching it.

Breaking up a bar fight in the back of beyond is not my place. Knocking back the final swigs of my 'one for the road' the firewater simultaneously burns and numbs my throat as it slides down. I've had about as much as I can take. I climb to my feet ready to unravel a note for the old timer. Without even a word spoken I spin ready to make my leave. The bar had just gotten a whole lot too crowded. The three fools roughing up Cherry at the bar barely register my footfall on the hardwood floor as the wails of the young lady drown them out. Her cheek is slammed and pinned against the counter by Denim's hand. He has an explosive temper. Heading for the door no eyes notice my exit except hers. They're wide and afraid and I can almost see the reflection of myself slip out of doors etched into her unforgiving pupils. Her desperate twinkle of hope leaving out of the door with me; her nose is bloody and her cheek raw. She'll be bruised in the morning, if she lasts that long. I finally realise that those men were the reason she smelled the way she did when I first got the whiff of her. This wasn't the first time she and they had crossed paths, but what interest is it of mine? Who am I to step into an argument? It isn't really my place is it?

***

Without the thunder the tempo of the night is cooler outside the bar than in. The rain tastes every bit as salty as Cherry's skin smells. The thought of those bastards tenderising such a fresh fillet of meat without the mildest bit of seasoning agitates my moral fibre. Moping by my car in the blackest corner of the car park I throw in my keys and leather. I should have smashed that hole to hell, introduced my boot to Denim's face but I still need one more look at that little brunette before I can leave satisfied; before I can climb in my stead and speed away. Standing out in the rain accepting the surge of rainwater wash over me; letting it drop off the tips of the hair that hangs over my face goes a long way from pacifying my mood. The wet squalor surging between my toes does little to convince me to leave. I grind my nails into my palms. All I can do is to wait; my impatience drawing blood. The same salty air escapes out of my nostrils as I breathe the torrid current flowing out like a pressure gauge. Tasting the anger on my tongue, I've already bitten down on my lip, my blood baited at curdling point. When and how did I allow that Cherry babe to get under my skin? I stand like a fool out in the rain waiting for one more look; one more smell. Creeping in the dark space beside my car, I focus on the distance between me and the door to The Hell Hole, subconsciously counting every single raindrop. I'm still curious as to what's going to happen next...

Within no time Cherry rushes out of the doors or more like she is exited out, real fast and backward. She falls backwards on her ass out into the rain the back of her soaked through. This one's a fighter though; she's scrambling to her feet. The burst of air that follows her already tastes of old pennies, bloody from her wounds. The three creeps' hands are on her dragging her through yet another puddle till their feet kick her down into another; Denim's hands bloody though getting rinsed clean drop by drop by the rain. She's a wild eyed beauty queen and they're all but ready to de-crown her. They're edging her over to the souped-up monstrosity that passes for their ride. There is only one way that this is going to play out once they get her inside and it's up to them whether she lives to see the dawn.

Their motor is flashy orange with blue racing stripes down the sides. I suddenly find myself in the mood to repaint those stripes; red seeming the most appropriate choice of colour. The anger swells up inside of me and in a twist of fur and fury the first one doesn't even see me coming. I'm on the cowboy first tearing him up and then I've thrown him off towards the bar before he has time to even holler. The second, the hairless monkey starts to turn trying to steal another look at me but this time he will remember my face; my true face. Ready with a knife in his hand and fear in his eyes, his puny human reactions are no match for mine. I break bone and twist till I hear the satisfying thud of the knife hitting the ground and he's out cold. I swear I catch a brief glimpse of the beast in his eyes on his way down. The third, the prettiest of the three would have still remained that way if only he hadn't set foot in 'The Hell Hole' tonight of all nights. It's all too right, with the coward on his knees begging and pleading at the sight of me, as if that could stop me. He dribbles and whines that he's sorry and doesn't want to die yet and I have not even laid a finger on him. Yet...

His eyes daring to wander back to the pretty thing soaked to the bone knee-deep in a puddle of their choosing; the woman that started it all and his silly desire to possess her, he looks at her shocked, wanting nothing but absolution but that is not hers to give. I take hold of the thumb-suckers digit shaped pacifier; the one that tasted of Cherry's lips and crunch, it goes. He snivels through the pain. Denim doesn't know pain, but I'm willing to teach him all about it. The bones snap with the simplicity of a lead pencil. Without even a flinch I pause then slice at his cheeks till he wails louder than she did. She hasn't been so pathetic as to whine, snivel or grovel. With a blow to the gut and an uppercut he splatters back into his windscreen, the bonnet getting a fresh coating of blood red paint.

I let the rage flow out slowly enough to catch the change in me. The twisting muzzle reverts to the nose that I'm more used to. The warmth of my breath cascading around my face to a quieter peaceful breath, Cherry inhales sharply as she watches my every move. My teeth and talons retract to my man-sized versions. The fuzz of my flesh reverts to just the dirty unshaved stubble around my jaw. The soothing rainwater cascades from my pelt; over the curves of my back; there's always a hunger to kill in me but my thoughts are still mine. It's always been that way. I extend my hand to the little lady who is up to her knees in sludge. She's too tired to scream or fight. She puts her hand into mine willingly; it's soft, her knuckles bleeding, her blood smelling sweeter than her skin. Her painted nails match the trickle of blood as it works its way down her deliciously slender fingers, my favourite colour though I'm sure she now knows why that is.

Her legs turn to jelly, her spaghetti heels unsteady and caked in mud. To me she's curvy in all the right places the way a Spanish guitar should be. I want to take her everywhere with me, the way a travelling musician would. Every night I'll gladly get all hot and sweaty playing with her strings and making sweet notes till the sun comes up. Her face is a concoction of blood, sweat, rain and desert sand but she still remains the prettiest thing in my little corner of the world. Her eyes are wide and mysteriously green capturing the night just right and even as I reach to dab away the blood from her cheek she's neither wary nor jumpy at my touch. She's trembling and for the life of me I can't think of what to say except "Welcome to the Hell Hole".

THE GHOST OF STRAWBERRY HILL

DAVID CRAIG

I had been living in the halls of St. Mary's College, Twickenham for just over a month back in 1988 when the events I'm about to mention occurred.
    The college was set in the grounds of Horace Walpole's famous house in Strawberry Hill. He was an 18th Century socialite and writer of the first Gothic horror novel. He'd built the house, which is seen by many as a Gothic castle, in a number of varying architectural styles and it was the first of its kind in the world. The most striking part of the house, the Round Tower, was to become it's most macabre and portentous. It was said that Walpole was a necromancer and that he built the tower to be as close to perfectly round as possible, with window frames and glass to fit, purely because it was believed that this would provide the best conditions to be able to summon the devil.
    It didn't take long after starting my Classics and History degree at St. Mary's before I started hearing a number of terrifying stories linked to Walpole's house and the college that had been annexed to Strawberry Hill. Tales of strange deaths and bizarre suicides along with a number of wardens, who were Catholic priests, going insane after supposedly seeing terrifying sights, were all very quickly on the lips of most students. One name that kept cropping up was Lady Waldegrave. We were informed that she had killed two of her husbands and her own children in early Victorian times when she lived in the house after Walpole's death. It turned out that it was tradition within the college to go on a ghost hunt and search for Lady Waldegrave, who was supposedly known to appear on 23rd October, which was, I was told, the date of her own death.
So, on that night a large number of students prepared to meet and walk around the grounds of the college in hair-raising hope of seeing a ghost! The clocks had gone back the weekend before and the days were getting shorter so we met outside the church around 8pm when it was suitably dark. We headed off in groups of five or six, some with torches and others determined to stick to the dimly lit paths. All of a sudden, the famous fog from the Thames came rolling in and enveloped the grounds. This was particularly eerie as it was the first night that this had happened. Everyone's pulses started to race that little bit more. After five minutes or so I told my mates that I had had enough of ghost hunting and was going to walk over to see my girlfriend near Bushy Park instead. I headed off and left them to wander around in the thickening fog and disquieting darkness.
    The following morning I headed to the refectory for breakfast before my first lecture started. The whole place seemed to be full of dark murmurs and whispers. I sat

down and it seemed that everyone was talking about the ghost hunting the previous night.

"Did you hear it?" was what everyone seemed to be saying!

"Hear what?" I asked.

"Oh, yeah! You'd gone off to see Helen hadn't you!" exclaimed one of the lads:

> It was unbelievable man! Not long after you'd gone everyone suddenly heard this weird, spooky wailing sound. No one could tell where it was coming from and it seemed to be everywhere. I nearly shat myself!

"Don't be daft" I laughed, "what are you on about, a wailing sound?"

"No, he's right!" said another one of my mates, "I heard it. It was scary man, like a ghost crying in the fog. It was so eerie. I've never heard anything like it."

> Some people just ran away in fright and the girls, well, some were screaming! Most of us were just so shit scared we didn't say anything at all but just got out of there!

... gasped another lad.

It was the talk of the college for a week at least and when I met up with some of my mates on reunions that night was often mentioned and the lads said that they'd never been so scared.

Well, last year we had a reunion and I explained to the lads, with a cheeky grin, that I did go to my girlfriend's place on that unearthly night, but I didn't go straight there. When I walked off from the ghost hunt I waited until I was out of sight and then ran up to my room on the second floor. I went in but didn't turn the lights on and pulled up the old window frame and placed my Fender guitar amp on the ledge. Two days prior to this day of doom I'd gone to Denmark Street in London and purchased an E-Bow with part of my student grant. This is an electro-magnetic device that you place over the strings of a guitar and it vibrates the string producing a sound that may be described as the cry of a whale or indeed the wail of a ghost crying from the depths of hell! I plugged my guitar in and switched on my digital delay pedal to add echo to the sound and started playing the guitar with my new fiendish toy!

I could hear people crying out all of a sudden things like "What the f*** was that?" "Oh, shit, what's that?" "I'm getting out of here" and other similar phrases amongst the screams of the girls, and some of the boys!

My prank had worked a treat and the lads couldn't believe what I was telling them. I'll not repeat what they called me!

But that isn't the end of the story.

The night after that grisly ghost hunt I again went to see my girlfriend but came home earlier than usual as she had extra work to do. I walked back through Teddington and down Waldegrave Road to the College and headed for my halls. I entered my room and decided to have an early night so got sorted for bed. As I turned my light out I noticed that it seemed foggy again outside but it strangely seemed as if the fog was just outside my window and nowhere else. I discounted this and turned to close my eyes and try to get to sleep. I suddenly felt a chilling shiver all of the way through my body. I turned to get out of bed and close the window but stopped dead, frozen still before I even got a toe out from under the covers. At the bottom of my bed, looking directly at me with black rimmed menacing eyes was a wizened old woman dressed in what looked like a garish white night gown. She didn't move and neither did I at first. I couldn't believe what I was seeing! I was petrified at first but then did what any self respecting young lad would do in that situation. I pulled the covers over my head and hid!

I eventually peeked out from under the covers, my fingers almost white from gripping so tightly. There was nothing and nobody there anymore. I got up immediately. No one could have got into my room because the door was still locked and no one would have been able to climb up the wall to my room from outside because there was no drain pipe or anything to hold onto to.

All that I could think was that it had been Lady Waldegrave, the Ghost of Strawberry Hill, appearing to warn me after my antics the previous night!

THE DAMNED

KATIE MCMAHON

My mammy said 'for the love of God, she's nothing but an ugly man in a bad wig,
Like something out of them films
Them Hammer Horrors
Who would ever?'
And as night fell I found
When you don't have a stake, a hammer will do.

TEMPTATION

NICOLA ROOKS

Her glossy raven black hair caught the shaft of sunlight from the half drawn shade, despite it being pulled back into a severe bun. This only stood to emphasise the pale almost translucent beauty of her skin. Her full red lips and dark eyes intently studied the wooden floor she was meticulously cleaning. The Master's gaze travelled down over her hunched form focusing on the surprisingly voluptuous breasts on her slim frame, which were marvellously exposed as she went about her household chores. They did not seem to heave and jiggle as much as the other housemaids yet remained still almost as if she never took a breath. He could feel a familiar stirring in his breeches and the urge of wanting to take her virginity there and then grew almost unbearable. He coughed and she looked up at him but did not seem surprised by his close presence.
"Girl... What is your name?" he shouted at her unnerved by the mocking look in her eyes.
"Christina... Sir," the pause between her name and addressing him was audible. He could feel himself growing red.
"Stand up when you address your Master you slovenly wench you!"
She slowly raised herself to her feet and when her gaze matched his, the mocking look in those pools of black oil was gone.
"Sorry Sir," she barely whispered, "I am new here, please forgive me?" She cast her eyes downwards and he felt his anger dissipating but his ardour remained.
"Well Christina that is a strange name. Where does it come from?"

> I don't know Sir. I was adopted as a young child and when my adoptive parents died I had to look for work and luckily happened upon your great home where the Housekeeper informed me there was a vacancy for which I am very grateful.

She stopped speaking, seeming embarrassed at her verbal incontinence. The Master lifted her chin so her eyes once again met his. "I am sure there will be some way, somehow, someday, you can thank me." His rough fingers casually travelled down her pale elegant throat and brushed the raised mounds of her sallow skinned breasts, lingering for a few seconds, and then he swiftly turned and walked away, the heels of his riding boots loud against the polished wooden floor. Christina could barely contain the snarl deep from within her as the Master strode away. Her blood red lips curled over her immaculate sharp white teeth and her eyes turned scarlet as her anger continued to grow. She leant against the flock wallpaper and willed herself to be calm. After a few moments her eyes reverted back to their black marbles and she knelt back down and continued her domestic work.

The night air was cool but welcome against her skin. It lightly lifted her dark locks which were free from their restraining uniformed style. Her smooth pearl hands unlined, despite the hours kept in soapy water, ran over the gnarled bark of the upturned log she was sitting on at the entrance of the forest, which was at the back of the great house. She looked up, not at all surprised by the form standing next to her
"Hello Alexander." The dark figure, enclosed in a black cape, sat down beside her.
"Christina my dear, it has been a long, long time yet you somehow remain as beautiful and youthful as ever." He chuckled at his own joke.
"I am thirsty, very, very thirsty and the contents of this house smell so delightful."
"No!" Her voice was like a gunshot, "No please Alexander not here."
"But why my Dear? Don't be so greedy. Surely there is enough for both of us?"
Christina turned and studied him, his skin stretched so tight over his face you could almost see the bones underneath. He did look so very hungry but she just could not risk it. Everything she had worked so hard for just to be normal.
"No Alexander I do not feed here but find my sustenance in the forest. Please I beg you. Not here." Alexander arose, his great cape swirling around his tall form like a swarm of locusts. "My Dear only for you I will obey your wishes. I hope you come to your senses soon we have a lot of catching up to do." Christina blinked and he was gone. She stood up and made her way towards the house.

The Master watched Christina walk across the lawn, not even leaving an imprint in the grass from her heavy work boots. The evening breeze lifted her skirts exposing her shapely legs and slim ankles. He felt the stirring again. He dropped the heavy velvet curtains he was holding and they settled back into place against the large sash windows. This time he would be sated.
Christina knew it was time. She sighed. She had tried so hard for so long to resist. Shame he had not then his life may have been spared. As he walked towards her she slowed down. There was no point fighting fate. "Christina. I wonder if I may trouble you for your help in the barn." Wordlessly she turned towards the large outbuilding outlined against the night sky like a werewolf against a full moon. The Master hastily followed her. This was easy he thought. They normally put up a bit of a struggle. Her submission excited him further and he could feel his erection straining against his trousers.
The barn was barely lit but he could see her slim body against the hay bales which were stored there; her beautiful white skin opaque in the moonlight which shone through the slats on the shuttered windows. She remained still as he ran his hand down her full

décolletage. As his passion overtook his senses he ripped her bodice from her and grabbed her roughly. Her breasts free from their cloth restraints tumbled out and he could feel her erect nipples and in his haste he became clumsy and both predator and prey fell onto the hay behind them. His breathing became ragged and rough as Christina remained motionless. He clawed at her skirts and he ran his hands up her smooth legs and so intent on his purpose was he that he didn't notice her eyes become pools of swirling fire and her fangs growing menacingly over her snarling crimson lips. As he reached the top of her legs he stopped in surprise. She was icy cold, like his barren wife. Normally the warmth was what kept him going; what he wanted. What was going on? He lifted himself up and screamed as he saw the sight before him. Half naked, her black hair was wild framing a sheer white face; eyes as red as ripe cherries, she looked like a demon from Hell itself. He did not get time to utter a word as she sprang on his exposed neck and pierced his carotid artery the blood spurting satisfactorily all over her translucent skin. Within five minutes he was empty but her thirst was barely quenched. It was done. It was time. As she walked towards the great house Alexander joined her.

LAURA

MICHELLE McCABE

The clock tock-ticked, tock-ticked, towards a staccato like screech. I opened my eyes, wide and alert, and turned towards the offender. His face told me it was 3 am. I started to shiver. The room felt like a freezer and I could hear the sound of torrential rain, pounding against the large sash windows.

I rose from my bed and stumbled clumsily. I looked around at my surroundings. My bedroom was seemed so different. I had been living here for six months yet I still wasn't used to the large Victorian terraced house that I should, by now, be calling home.

I heard what sounded like a trapped bird, trying to escape from whichever prison was holding it. The offending shrieks seemed to be coming from behind an old dusty curtain which I hadn't got round to tearing down. I peeled it back tentatively to reveal an oaken door, gnarled and rotten; riddled with woodworm. The doorknob was stiff and cold to the touch but it served its purpose and slowly the old door creaked open and I crept through into the darkness.

I heard a shriek then realized it had come from my own lips. I smiled feeling a little silly that I had recoiled at the sight of my own reflection suddenly visible in an old dusty mirror which despite layers of filth was still capable of displaying plainly how my eyes had shrunken deep into their sockets.

Curious, I descended the stone staircase and stumbled into what appeared to be some sort of dungeon. The moon's rays seeped through a narrow window revealing huge rusty chains hanging high on the walls of this unwelcoming abode. I wondered what poor, unfortunate men or women had hung here for months or even years? And how many of them had died without seeing the light of day again?

As my eyes grew accustomed to the poor light I could see what looked like bones strewn all over the damp, stone floor; the putrid smell threatening to overwhelm me. I walked slowly, almost trance-like towards another ancient oak door which leered at me on the wall opposite the staircase. It opened spontaneously and to reveal a luscious, grandiose hallway, with deep pile red flamboyant carpet, which felt soft to my cold and wet feet. Beyond the hall, I could hear excited voices, chattering and giggling I peered into the darkness at the shadows which flickered across the walls, danced across the ceiling and merged into one mass of confusion.

"My dear Laura… welcome to my home. May I offer you a drink?"

Startled, I stared at the strange spectre who somehow knew my name. He handed me an ornate goblet containing what appeared to be red wine.

"May I have a glass of water?" I croaked pathetically; still not sure if I was actually awake. My throat was dry and my voice sounded cracked and fragile.

"But of course, Laura, come with me."

He led me into a library; the smell of foisty leather catching my breath. "Sit down, Laura."

"How do you know who I am?" I demanded, "… and why am I here?"

"You chose to come here" he explained softly.

Although my mind felt alert my thoughts were flying. My eyes were chasing images which at once appeared and then melted back as if in a Salvador Dali painting. Though a professed atheist I began to pray desperately.

My strange, new companion took me in his arms and pulled me closely to him. I could feel his cold breath on the side of my neck. My mind swirled. I felt as cold as ice; my heart was beating rapidly and loudly. The sound of my heartbeat pounded my ears. I wanted to scream but the muscles in my throat contracted preventing even the slightest of whispers being released.

I could hear pipe music; a fast, furious polka as my unrequited partner laughing hysterically swirled me round and round, flinging me effortlessly back and forth

Suddenly the flickering candle light caught the silver of my necklace. The spectre winced as he shrank away from my Grandmother's crucifix which I'd worn since she passed away.

"Laura, come towards me my Darling."

She gently took my hand and led me away. As I returned to my bedroom my Grandmother had gone.

A gentle breeze passed through me; I shivered and fell onto my bed.

WHITE

KIRSTIE GROOM

I have always known that this world was filled with such evil that even the best of us cannot escape.

When I was a child, I was attacked by a demon, which was hiding in the body of a man - my Father. I was too young to understand it then, but, as I grew older, I began to piece it together, like replacing pages torn from a book. My Father was possessed, and the demon made him hurt me, forced him to touch me in ways that only a man and wife should touch. I mostly only remember it in vague, dreamlike images and sounds that haunt my memories. Some parts are more vivid, and I wish I could forget them too, but the sisters at St. Michael's Convent have reminded me, daily, of what that demon took away from me, how it destroyed my innocence, my purity, and my parents.

My Mother caught him one night after he had taken me up to my bedroom. The door burst open, and then they were screaming at each other. I don't know what they said, I just remember noise, and tears flooding my face, cascading from my chin onto my bare legs. My Father grabbed at her arms, but she wouldn't let him touch her; she must have known about the demon. She ran away, down the stairs and into the kitchen below. My Father chased her. More noise. I crept out onto the landing, and pressed my face up against the banister, clinging to the spindles as if they were all that was keeping me rooted to that spot. I could see them through the gaps. My Mother was sobbing at the kitchen sink, as my Father crooned over her in sickly sweet tones, but all she could do was cry and shout "No!"

I don't know how long this went on, but in my hazy memory it seems like hours of them shouting, pleading, crying, and of me just watching it go on, like a film replaying over and over on a loop. Eventually my Mother snapped, filling with strength I had never seen in her before. She lunged at my Father - fists flying, teeth bared. She collided with him, knocking him to the floor. Blood splattered his cheek where the skin split with the sheer force of her attack. I clenched my eyes tight shut. Noise again: screaming and crying and shouting, snarling, vicious sounds like animals tearing each other to shreds; a thud and a clatter.

Silence.

I kept my eyes closed, my fingers still wrapped around the banister so tightly I imagined I was leaving dents in the solid wood.
'Mummy?' I called out to her, but she didn't answer me. I kept calling.
Eventually, I opened my eyes. My Mother lay on her side, knees pressed tightly to her chest, arms wrapped around them. I thought she was sleeping, and so ran down the stairs to waken her. Deep crimson spattered her arms and face, marring her perfect creamy skin. Tears dripped silently from her glassy, unblinking eyes, tracking glimmering lines along her cheekbones until they mingled with the blood that was dripping onto the floor from a cut in her head. I wanted to wipe it all away and make her beautiful again so she wouldn't be this lifeless rag doll with dead eyes anymore. But, in the same moment, I was afraid to touch her; I didn't want the red to coat my hands like it had hers. She was staring straight through me, as if I was invisible, like I sometimes pretended to be when I was alone with my Father.

I went to him; he lay near my Mother. His eyes were half closed, his mouth slack, his chest still. I knelt down beside him, gingerly reaching out one chubby arm to nudge him awake. He didn't move. I shook him harder; his head lolled from side to side, like a puppet with a loose string, and his arm, which was red like my Mother's hands, flopped from his chest to the floor, making a quiet slap as it landed. That's when I noticed the blood, pooling around him, spreading out across the checkerboard linoleum from a patch on his ribs that was as dark as the black squares.

I skittered back towards my Mother, my feet streaking blood along the floor. My choked sob shattered the silence, as I forced my way under her arms into an uncomfortable embrace burying my face into her chest. I hated to see my Mother cry. We lay there for what seemed like forever, her dark hair tickling my face, and her chest shaking with ragged sobs. Her perfume was faint, masked under the sour musk of stale sweat, but it was still there, sweet, floral and delicate. It was everything she was, or rather, used to be. I waited for her to comfort me, wishing she would whisper my name in her soft voice like she did when I woke up, screaming, from a nightmare: "Shh, it's okay, Anna. I'm here".

She didn't make a sound.

Sirens began to swell outside. Loud male voices joined them. Heavy footfalls echoed around me, and the men muttered to each other.
"He's gone."
"Are they?"
Warm breath tickled my shoulder, as one of them leaned over me to touch my Mother's neck, and then mine.
"Both fine."

Rough hands lifted me from my Mother's side, carrying me like a baby. I could see my parents still, lying on the floor, surrounded by black clad men with grim faces. I kept watching them, until we passed through the splintered door frame, into the cold December wind outside.

***

That was the last time I saw them, before I was sent to live at the Convent. The Sisters helped me to understand what had happened to my Father, how his lack of faith had given the demon access to his body; he had become the monster that lived inside him, rotting from the inside out. When I was younger, I couldn't understand why I wasn't allowed to see my Mother, but I know better now. When she killed my Father she gave in to sin, her despair allowed wrath to consume her, and for that she had to go away. I can't guess where she is now, or if she's even still alive. After everything I've learned, I don't want to know.

When they found me, I needed special care. My body had to be purified, and my soul had to be cleansed. I don't know what they did, but it left me with ability uncommon amongst God's creatures. Now I can see things for what they really are. The sins that people have committed are as visible as the colour of their hair, or clothes. It took time for me to realise. For most of my life I never left the Convent, everyone there was the same. A faint white outline shimmered around their bodies; I never knew anything different until I was exposed to the world outside for the first time. It was filled with colour. Not in the bright and joyful sense you might imagine, I knew even then that there was something inherently bad in these auras, as I later learned to call them. Blue, green, gold, orange, pink, purple, red, that's all I see when I look out into the world now. The only white left is in the Convent, and in the children that are dragged around by these monsters.

***

I see them now, milling around this busy city, colours glowing like the Christmas lights that are strung up on every building and lamp post. They are sick, disgusting, and yet, every day, I watch the people inside that colourful glow trudge down the street, going about their lives, as if they're doing nothing wrong. They're dripping with it - their sin - and this world is full of them: dying souls, too weak, too faithless, to resist temptation. I shiver as they brush past me, and though the December wind is icy, it is nothing compared to the chill of evil that emanates from their bodies.

Blue, under the monument; he might as well be frozen to the ground. He doesn't move. He just lies under his tattered old coat, shamelessly wasting his life away. He doesn't seem to know that I can see that smirk under his unkempt facial hair, and the wrinkled laughter lines hiding beneath the grime on his face.

Green is everywhere, spreading like bacteria, multiplying and reproducing in a single thought, infecting the nation with its sickly hue. It watches everyone, never satisfied with its lot. Green throws acid in the face of a beautiful girl. Green scorns the young. Green destroys happy couples. Green is bitter, twisted, and almost never alone.

Gold follows green, hoarding money and material possessions. Gold fills the front pages of newspapers with its pompous grin, as the taxpayers unknowingly fund his luxury holiday to Dubai, and his children's private school education, whilst they can barely afford to feed their own families. Gold is lusting after the clothes in the windows of the designer boutiques, and gold is counting up the profits on the cheap products with the expensive labels. Gold owns the shops and the restaurants. Gold governs the world.

Orange queues outside the hot dog van, the cake shop, the McDonald's, and the KFC. Rolls of skin and fat undulate as he reaches around his protruding stomach into his pockets to pay for the food he doesn't need to eat. Orange stuffs her face with sweets at the bus stop, placating her child with crisps in place of love and attention. Orange is everywhere, eating itself to death, unable to admit that the fault is its own. It blocks up paths and doorways like grease clogs a drain, suffocating the pipework of the city centre.

Pink can always be found stumbling out of a bar at closing time, an unsuspecting man hanging off her arm, and her every word. She takes away their inhibitions with alcohol and well directed compliments, and makes them forget they have wives who remain faithful to them at home by beckoning them to share her rosé coloured glow. She skulks out of cheap hotel rooms in the middle of the night, satisfied, and shamefully guiltless. Pink tempts weak men with her revealing clothes, and vulgar flirtation. Pink destroys families, and leads to other sins; green and red.

Worst is purple, conceited and self-important. It glares down at the rest of us from billboards and TV screens. Purple sneers at everything and everyone, at orange, and blue, and pink. Faultless in its own eyes, purple sees no wrong even in its failings. It is ever reaching, and ever climbing, determined to be higher than everyone, higher even than God.

Last is red. Red can flare up anywhere. It bursts out of people, unexpected. It bruises and bloodies. Red is all consuming, and destructive, breaking bones and battering bodies. It is assault and murder. Red is my only memory of my Mother.

They are everywhere, daring me to destroy them, to end this world that is filled with decay and entropy. But I won't fall into their trap. I have to find a way to use this gift without becoming one of them. I pray for a sign, willing God to answer me. I kneel in the street, the cracked pavement freezing welts into my shins. The rush of swirling colour around me halts and, even as I close my eyes in prayer, I can feel them glaring at me, their twisted faces looming closer as I mutter each word under my breath, but I won't stop until I have my answer. I twist my rosary around my fingers, my ungloved hand as white as the beads. The silver crucifix punctures my palm smearing the minute figure of Christ with my blood. The crowd chatters, desperately trying to distract me. Someone tries to pull me to my feet, but I am unyielding. I speak aloud, letting them hear my prayer. They curse me, crying at me to stop. The noise reaches a crescendo, and a cry rips through my body, as a booming voice shouts: "Enough!"

    I am startled by white light, as my head collides with the ground, and my eyes flutter open. The pedestrian traffic continues as if nothing has happened. They rush in and out of shops, gathering their Christmas shopping. I pull myself up from the ground, as bizarre white flecks descend from the grey sky. I hold out my hand to catch one as it falls, it is tiny and perfect: a moment of pristine purity that is lost in an instant. More tiny flakes land in my palm, mingling with the red blood that weeps from my stinging wounds.

    Suddenly I understand. I can see the message that I have been given. I am mutable, and fragile: I am the snow, and corruption is coming for me. I snatch up my blood-stained rosary from the floor, and run.

The Inn

Jamie Spears

The stagecoach bounced and rattled along the snow-covered path. The passengers winced as the wooden wheels crashed over every rock and branch in its path.

"Almost there *Mesdames, Monsieur*," called the coach driver from his perch: "I can see the inn from here!"

The Scientist pushed open the window on his side, filling the carriage with a gust of sharp, cold air. "It is a grand old building", he remarked, approvingly.

The Heiress reached over and snapped the window shut. "I shouldn't like to die from pneumonia for the sake of a grand building, *Monsieur*."

He touched the brim of his hat. "My apologies, *Madame*."

The inn stood alone, a huge, imposing figure at the edge of St Jovite. It had been built some two hundred years before, as a home for a wealthy colonel in the British army, following his side's victory in *la guerre de la conquête*. As the centuries passed, the family and their home had both fallen into disrepute.

Madame Hubert had been in possession of the house for ten years, ever since the death of Monsieur Hubert (thus making fine use of the logging company's compensation). She operated it as an inn for the stagecoach passengers making the arduous journey across Québec.

As the coach neared the inn, Madame Hubert stepped onto the porch to greet her passengers. First out was the beautifully attired Heiress. Ignoring the coach driver's hand, she alighted and looked for a moment at her surroundings. With an eye roll of contempt, she moved quickly for the front door of the inn, calling out a warning that her valises were not to be scratched. Next was the exceptionally white-faced Cécile. Eyes firmly downcast, she bid a polite, if quiet, good evening to both the coach driver and Madame Hubert. The Scientist was last out, insisting that Madame Hubert give him the detailed history of the inn. Assuring him that she would, Madame Hubert ushered him inside to join the rest of the party.

***

The Scientist nodded in the direction of Cécile, "She is afraid".
"Do you know much about her?" asked Madame Hubert.

"She only joined the coach at Ste-Agathe", the Scientist replied, "and barely spoke but to bid us a good morning".
"She looks so young. Perhaps she is away from her family for the first time."
"Perhaps."
The Heiress entered and took up the vacant seat next to the Scientist, distracting the innkeeper from her pity for the young Cécile.
"Am I to understand, *Madame*, that you have given me the best room in the house?"
"I have *Madame*. Is it not to your satisfaction?"
"I suppose it will suffice for one night," she sniffed, "I shall be extremely grateful to get to civilisation in Montréal. I don't know how you people manage in these conditions".
Madame Hubert smiled her greasiest smile of mock-contrition:

> St Jovite is flourishing, my dear *Madame*. Very soon it will rival Montréal in terms of amenities. But for now, I regret, you may have the choice of these rooms, or the barn with the horses. Now, I believe dinner is ready, if you'd like to follow me into the dining room.

The Heiress and the Scientist vacated their chairs by the fire, and exited the sitting room. Cécile remained, stood by the window, looking out at the snowdrifts that extended for miles beyond view.
"*Mademoiselle?*" inquired Madame Hubert. Cécile turned, and without speaking, followed the group to dinner.

***

The trio of travellers sat at the table, as Madame Hubert placed their *entrées* on the table. She noticed a broad grin on Cécile's face.
"Is everything all right?" asked Madame Hubert.
Cécile's grin remained painted on her face as she nodded in the affirmative. She sat, still smiling, as the three began to eat.
"My dear", began Madame Hubert, "you've hardly touched your food. Is anything the matter?"
Cécile started to laugh—a harsh, barking laugh that caused the Heiress to drop her fork to the floor. "It doesn't matter!" she cried, "It doesn't matter! I am going to die tonight!"
The Heiress gasped. Madame Hubert blessed herself. The Scientist calmly put down his fork, and asked, "my dear, what makes you think that?"

Cécile let forth another burst of high-pitched laughter, "I will never leave this house. I will die tonight! And you, *you*, will have killed me!"

"Who is going to kill you?"

"You, my fellow travellers. You will be responsible for my death tonight."

"You spiteful, horrible, girl!" hissed the Heiress, "How dare you say something like that. *Madame*", she turned to Madame Hubert, "you should turn this hateful thing from your house!"

The Scientist held up a hand. "Now Cécile, have you had fever recently? Or perhaps an injury—maybe a fall in a riding accident?"

"No."

"Perhaps you are feeling frightened to be away from home for the first time?"

"I'm not frightened to be away from home. I am frightened to die."

The Heiress stood up from the table with such force that her chair was knocked over. "*Madame*, I must insist that you remove this girl!"

Madame Hubert stood and ushered the girl, her eyes still shining with an unholy brightness, from the dining room and into the kitchen. She uncorked a bottle of whiskey and poured two measures. She pushed one of the tumblers towards Cécile before downing her own in one gulp. "Drink, my dear", implored Madame Hubert, "Drink and it will calm your nerves".

Cécile took one small sip, and winced at its harsh taste. "Finish the glass", encouraged Madame Hubert, not unkindly. Cécile drained the glass and gingerly placed it on the table. Madame Hubert reached again for the bottle. "Have another one", she said as she poured. And again the two women drank.

"How do you feel now?"

"A bit... flushed".

"But do you feel calm, my Dear?"

"Yes. I suppose I do".

"Good."

Madam Hubert re-corked the bottle and placed the used glasses by the sink, "You were frightening us with all that talk of dying".

"I didn't mean to frighten anyone. I just have this feeling..."

"This is your first time away from home? Away from your parents?"

"Yes."

"Then that's it. I expect you're just nervous and homesick. We'll have no more talk of dying tonight."

"Yes, *Madame*. I am sorry to have caused such a commotion."

"Think nothing of it, my Dear."

***

Back at the table, emboldened by the whiskey, Cécile explained that she was to be taking up the post of Governess to a wealthy family in Montréal. They were relations of family vaguely known to Cécile's Mother—but unknown to Cécile herself. She admitted her trepidation at taking the position, not least because it was so far from home.
"Well", said the Heiress when Cécile had finished recounting her story, "there is absolutely no reason to be worried. I shall give you my address, and you may call on me in Montréal next week".
"I shouldn't like to impose, *Madame*."
"Nonsense", said the Heiress with an imperious wave of the hand, "and I shall introduce you to my dressmaker. She is the finest one outside of New York".
The Scientist raised his glass in a toast: "o new friends".

***

Once dinner had finished, the three travellers made their way back to the sitting room. Sitting by the fire, the Scientist engrossed himself in a newspaper, and the Heiress took up her knitting. Cécile, though calmer than she had been at dinner, resumed her place by the window, and continued her surveying of the snowdrifts.
  There had been no fresh snow that day, but the wind whipped up the loose powder atop the mounds, and gave the impression that it was still falling from the sky.
  Madame Hubert bustled in with a tray of coffees, and placed it on the small table near the fire, "Cécile, please join us".
Almost reluctantly, Cécile tore herself away from the window and took up a chair by the fire, next to the Heiress.
"What were you looking at?" asked Madame Hubert, as she handed her a cup of coffee.
'Nothing.'
"Of course it was nothing", interjected the Heiress, "it's pitch black! You couldn't possibly see anything without a lantern".
"I have a feeling that another is coming. Another will be joining us. But he's waiting."
The Heiress scoffed. The Scientist, fearing a reprisal of the dinner-time hysterics, suggested a game, "Bridge, ladies? Or Rummy?"
"I have just the thing!" gasped the Heiress, "Just wait here, it's upstairs, in my case".
The two remaining travellers and Madame Hubert sat sipping their coffees as they watched the Heiress dash from the room.
"What do you think it could be?" asked Madame Hubert.

"I expect it's one of the games favoured by the fashionable ladies of the *cité*." The Scientist turned to Cécile with a friendly smile, "you'd do well to pay attention here, if you want to fit in in Montréal".

Cécile returned the smile, "I hope the rules aren't too complicated".

I have it!" the Heiress announced as she burst back into the sitting room. She was carrying a wooden box, with a scrap of dark purple muslin thrown over it. Ignoring Madame Hubert's sputtered protests, she put the coffee tray on the floor before gently placing the box on the table in its stead. "Arrange your chairs around the table", she ordered, and the three obeyed. Satisfied she had their full attention, she pulled the muslin off the top of the box. With the delicacy of a surgeon, she opened the box, revealing the heart-shaped board it contained.

"There!" she said triumphantly, standing back from the table.

"What is it?" asked Madame Hubert.

"It's a planchette" answered the Heiress, though she was disappointed by the rather blank expressions on the faces of her company. "A planchette", she repeated, "we can use it to speak to the spirits".

Once again that evening, Madame Hubert had cause to bless herself. "*Que Dieu nous garde*", she whispered.

"Yes I think I've heard of these,' said the Scientist, as he laid his hand atop the board, "They're quite fashionable with the genteel ladies of Paris, I believe".

"Yes they are", said the Heiress, shooing his hand from the board, "All over Europe they are used, even by Queen Victoria! It's very simple" she said, taking her seat, and placing a scrap of paper beneath the wheeled board, "We ask questions, and if there are any spirits around, they will respond by moving my hand like so". She demonstrated by moving the board to and fro over the paper.

"Ideomotor action" said the Scientist, "That's all it is".

"Perhaps. Have you ever seen it demonstrated in person, *Monsieur*?"

"I have not."

"It seems foolish to pass on an opportunity, *Monsieur le Scientifique*, to examine the phenomena for yourself. Have you got a pen, Monsieur?"

The Scientist reached into his breast pocket and handed the Heiress his pen. She placed it in the hole at the pointed end of the board, and rested her hands on the broad end opposite it. "Ask something" said the Heiress.

"Spirit!" he called out, "Spirit are you with us now?"

'I don't like this,' said Madame Hubert, as she clutched Cécile's hand.

"Don't worry, *Madame*. It's simply involuntary physiognomic movement on the part of the one controlling the board; a muscle spasm, by another name." He called out again, "Spirit! Spirit if you are…"

"Look!", Madame Hubert pointed at the board.

The planchette had begun to move. When the board came to a halt, the Heiress lifted it from the page, "*Oui*" she read.

"Yes, there is a spirit here", said the Scientist. "Well I certainly hope I have the honour of speaking to one of the good spirits?" This time the planchette spelt out "*Non*".

"Ah, a shame… is this one of Satan's many minions then?"

The board shot out from under the Heiress's hands, and began to fly around the table, scrawling hastily, "What does it say?" she asked, breathlessly.

"Almost", replied the Scientist, "It is writing 'almost'"

"Enough, enough!" shrieked Madame Hubert, "Please stop this at once!"

"I told you, *Madame*, it is simply small muscle movements in the hand of the controller that causes it to move. There is nothing supernatural here."

"But it moved without her hand!"

"It must be magnets attached to the underside of the board."

"There are no magnets,' said the Heiress, lifting the board to show the Scientist. He leant forward, brushing his fingers across the planchette, "It is a thick wood, there must be magnets embedded within the board. That is the only explanation".

The Heiress replaced the board on the table, "Even if there were magnets, *Monsieur*, how could they possibly spell out a word?"

For the first time that evening, the Scientist was unsure of himself:

> There must be an explanation; whether by deceit at the hands of our medium, or some form of magnets or currents that causes that planchette to move so.

"We'll have another go", said the Heiress, "ask a question".

"'Almost'… what?" asked the Scientist, "What does that mean?"

"I know", whispered Cécile, as once again, without the intervention of the Heiress, the planchette spun around on the page.

"What do you know?" asked Madame Hubert.

'I know it. I know it."

"I've got it", the Scientist said after a few moments, "I've got it. It's saying 'almost here'".

The fire began to flicker, as though it were in danger of going out.

"It's nearly here", said Cécile.

"That's just the wind. It's coming down the chimney and blowing the fire about", retorted the Scientist.

Suddenly a loud crash from upstairs shook the room. The Heiress and Madame Hubert shrieked in unison. The Scientist leapt to his feet and grabbed a poker from beside the fire. He walked over to the sitting room door and shut it.

The planchette had begun to spin again. Cécile stood over the board and looked at the paper beneath it.

"He's here", she said, "He's here".

The Scientist returned to the table, pulled the paper from under the board and threw it into the still-flickering fire. "No more of this!" he shouted, brandishing the poker at the Heiress. "I don't know what sort of trick you're playing here, *Madame*, but you are frightening the other ladies. This must stop at once!"

"This has never happened before, *Monsieur*. I don't… I don't understand this! It is just a game we play!" The Heiress sank down lower into her chair and fanned her face with her handkerchief. "I am so sorry, *Mesdames*, *Monsieur*. I don't know what has happened".

"Nonsense!" shouted the Scientist:

> We have not brought anything forth! There is *nothing* to bring forth! This is a trick you are playing, *Madame*, and for the sake of the other ladies, I urge you…

Three loud thumps were heard overhead. The entire party stopped, and looked up at the ceiling, "I think it's moving toward the stairs", whispered Madame Hubert. They listened in silence as the thumping noise, the supposed footfalls, appeared to be crossing from the bedroom overhead, toward the stairs. There was a loud creak as it reached the top of the stairs.

The footsteps started slowly to descend the stairs, with an incredibly heavy gait. When it reached the bottom of the stairs, it stopped. The Scientist crept back over towards the door and raised the poker, ready to strike the intruder.

The heavy footsteps resumed moving toward the sitting room door. The Scientist gripped the poker tighter, as the ladies stepped further and further back, toward to the dining room door at the opposite end of the room.

The door handle rattled, and the Heiress gasped loudly. The Scientist leaned his body against the door in an attempt to prevent the thing entering. The handle continued to rattle, and the Scientist felt the door push against him.

"Madame Hubert?' they heard from the hall, "It knows my name!"

"Madame Hubert? It's Urbain. Are you in the sitting room?"

She ran to the door and called out to the stablehand, "Urbain, Urbain, you must come in. Quickly! There is something out there!"

She pushed aside the Scientist and flung open the door, "Come in; come in". She grabbed the young man's arm and dragged him into the room behind her. He glanced around the room at the terrified women, and the now-bedraggled Scientist wielding a blunt instrument. "Is something the matter, *Madame*?" he asked, eyeing the Scientist with suspicion.

"Didn't you hear it?! Didn't you see it in the hall?"
"See what, *Madame*?"
"Something... Someone was coming down the stairs; coming toward this room!"
"I saw nothing *Madame*. And there is no one out there."
The Scientist pushed past Urbain, poker still in hand, "There's nothing here", he called back. He re-entered the room and deposited the poker back by the fireplace, "Were you on the stairs, boy?"

No, *Monsieur*. I only just entered to tell Madame Hubert that we're nearly out of fresh water for the horses. I was hoping to get some from the pump in the kitchen.

Madame Hubert composed herself, best as she could, "Of course, Urbain".
Cécile and the Heiress joined the Scientist by the fireplace and sat down heavily in the chairs. "Shall I box this for you Madam?" asked the Scientist, picking up the planchette.
She shook her head, "Throw it on the fire, *Monsieur*".

***

The party awoke early the next morning, to prepare for the final leg of their journey.
Madame Hubert was setting the dining room table as the Scientist walked in.
"Good morning, *Monsieur*."
"Good morning."
"I hope you slept well?"
"I did, *Madame*, thank you."
"Please do sit and begin your breakfast. I'll go see if the ladies are awake."
Madame Hubert crossed from the dining room into the siting room and realised that the chairs were still clustered around the table by the fire. She went to pull them away, and noticed that part of the planchette was still in the hearth, having failed to burn the night before. Picking up the poker she shoved it further into the fireplace, hoping the next time she lit a fire there, it would burn.

Climbing the stairs on her way to the bedrooms, she passed the Heiress. They exchanged pleasantries, and Madame Hubert told her that the Scientist had already made his way downstairs.
Madame Hubert continued on to Cécile's room. She knocked, but there was no reply.
"Cécile? It's Madame Hubert. Are you awake?"
Still nothing. Madame Hubert put her hand to the latch, and pushed it gently. It was unlocked and gave way instantly.
"I'm sorry to intrude, my dear Cécile, but..."

Madame Hubert screamed, and fell to the floor in a faint.

***

It was Spring, and the snow had finally melted.

The Scientist walked through the Place Jacques-Cartier, admiring its fashionable new buildings. He looked down at a scrap of paper in his hand, satisfied that he was at the correct address. He ascended the few steps in front of the house, and rang the bell. He turned around and admired the view for a moment: the sun shining beautifully over the river, as boats glided past.

"*Oui, Monsieur?*"

He handed the maid one of his cards, "I am a new friend of your mistress".

She bade him follow her into the house, and to wait in the foyer. The Scientist admired the lush carpeting on the stairs, and the sable, floral print of the wallpaper. After a few minutes, the Maid reappeared, and told him to follow her into the receiving room.

"*Monsieur!*" cried the Heiress as the Scientist entered, "I had not expected to see you!"

"I am sorry to intrude, *Madame*, but I had hoped to speak to you about a rather pressing matter."

"Yes, of course. Would you like tea or coffee?"

"No, thank you."

"A glass of wine, then?"

"No, no thank you, *Madame*."

He sat down on the settee opposite her, "If you wouldn't mind dismissing your maid?"

"Of course. Thank you, Marie." The Maid curtseyed and made her way silently from the room.

"*Madame*", he began, uneasily, "You remember that night we spent at the Inn in St Jovite, I trust?"

"Oh, you haven't come here just to remind me of that ghastly incident?"

> I regret to say I have. An acquaintance of mine is a doctor out in those parts. He wrote to tell me of the local innkeeper, a Madame Hubert. Apparently—and I am sorry if this news distresses you—she has died.

"A shame."

'Yes, and I… I wonder if it is not yet more blood on our hands.'

"Our hands? We have done nothing *Monsieur*! What had we to do with that girl's decision to…' the Heiress's voice dropped to a whisper, "destroy herself".

"She knew she was going to die. The girl, Cécile, she said she would die that night. And that we would be responsible."

"We were not responsible. The girl was homesick and frightened and probably mad! It was nothing to do with us."

> We brought forth the spirit that killed her. It somehow—I don't know—bored its way into her soul. Whatever came forth that night came for her. Perhaps it sensed she was weak, perhaps it sensed her fear. I cannot say. The answer exists beyond my knowledge.

"I thought you didn't believe in the spirits."

> If my thirty years as a practitioner of the sciences has taught me but one thing, it is that we are not to ignore our senses. I know what I heard and I know what I saw that night. We brought something forth, and it killed her.

> We didn't. We couldn't have. My friends and I played with the planchette many times, and nothing ever happened. It was just a bit of fun. I refuse to accept *any* blame in either death, *Monsieur*, and I'll thank you leave my house at once.

The Heiress stood and stalked to the door. As she opened it and spun around to face him, the Scientist saw that her face was flushed.
"I do apologise if I've cause you any undue anxiety, *Madame*", said the Scientist as he rose from the settee and walked past her out of the receiving room, "but the facts remain. We brought a spirit into our world from the next. We fulfilled Céline's premonition. We killed her".
The Heiress slammed the receiving room door in the Scientist's face.
The Scientist collected his coat from the Maid, and tipped his hat gallantly to her as he exited the Heiress's home. As he stepped out into the broad, new streets, he felt a slight chill in the air. He looked up, and saw that the Spring sun had vanished, to be replaced by thick, woolly clouds.

Last Call

Elizabeth Hazlett

I walk with purpose, to the bathroom,
Quick, yet slow, painful yet painless.
I lean against the sink, waiting, hoping,
To see my beauty. I look up-NO!
Not yet! Not quite! A-ha! There,
My blonde curls caress my face,
Shimmering in golden rays.
My eyes a beautiful hue of soulful meaning.
The lashes reach out to me…
Like a butterfly escaping.
My lips as red as carnations
Full of lustful promise.
But NO!
My hair.
Grey.
My eyes lifeless and dull…

'Norma! Norma! Where are you?'
Oh! Scared little girl, so fragile…
Why? Don't go! Don't go…
I need my Mogadon…to sleep.
But they need me! Just one more to go.
My contract ends soon.
A-ha! There again, my diamonds twinkle,
Against my flawless skin.
He notices! He always notices, does Kennedy.
To take me, want me, devour me,
Ruin and spoil my beauty.

I rest my head on the lavish pillow!
Seemingly uncomfortable old, musty…
But no, I can see their silk.
They must be silk! Just a couple
More pills I think! I don't reach them,
My dry, poor bones.
I'll speak to the press on Monday…
To stop it all. Make them stop.

It must be done; it must.
I cannot lose now. I must fight.
Ahh, the pain again!!! Oh, scared
Little Norma-what's happening?
So beautiful, so fragile…
I'm drifting, drifting off, sinking
Into the pillow. The telephone beside
The pills! I don't know.
I see the falls; I see Niagara…
A memorable moment.
'Arthur! Where are you?'
They may get me….
Get me…
'Diamonds are a girls…'
Will they remember, will they know?
The pain! Oh, my stomach is so empty!
Empty! Rancid! Wretched! Horrid!
Just like the little fostered girl,
Masked in cruel beauty.
They will get me. The pills help.
But don't. No Norma, don't go!
Help me, help me,
Help me…
The last waves of anguish terrorise me…
Everything goes black,
His eyes my last earthly sight.

SHADOWRAITH

STEVE WILLIS

I watch.
I wait.
Many years have passed since I saw you:
a shadow amongst shadows;
alive against the cobalt blue of early evening.
The heavily garmented trees soak up the day.
Heading for slumber you wait to feed on their life force,
transforming them into your minions;
your sentinels in the darkness.
My bedroom looks upon your battleground.
I watch.
I wait.
The church lies shrouded; darkness in a realm of hope.
But I feel you there hidden from sight,
waiting to reveal your power.

So I watch and I wait.
In the midnight blue of the witching hour,
we continue to play our game.
Light encroaches on night.
On Pegasus wings dawn approaches.
My eyes begin to flicker,
the exhaustion of my vigil calling me to slumber.
Soon I will return to see you again.
Always watching, always waiting,
a guardian of the light;
hunting for the wraith who mocks my fear.

I climb tiredly onto my bike, 6 p.m. Friday night. Twelve hours of boring monotonous drudgery finally behind me. Weariness in every pore I begin the trek home. Pedals slowly turning, my feet churn through each exhausted cycle, drawing me ever closer. The relief I feel on reaching the half mile steep hill leading down towards my household, hurts almost as much as the ride itself.

Pedals turning faster and faster, feet struggling to hold the pace, a wild grin creases my face. Memories flash, a young boy racing down this hill, wild war like cries splitting the night. Holding a crazy smile I thunder toward the village; my own reckless abandon spurring me homeward. Two sharp rights at breakneck speed; knees grazing tarmac I am catapulted into the street carrying enough momentum to reach home.

Not seeing my parents for a few days has made me realise I am working too much. Sixty or seventy hour weeks are not really good for the mind or the body. I have immersed myself in work as a layman's answer to pain management. The bitch I married had slunk back to her ex-boyfriend, leaving me to pack for home. Work seemed a sensible answer but in truth it's a coward's answer to loneliness. My parents' smiles dispel some of my weariness and ease my bitter hatred of life.

Wolfing down my food, I quietly mutter pleasantries to Mam and Dad and head for the shower. Thank heavens for power showers. Needle like jets of water acupuncture my tired, aching muscles, refreshing me. A night in the local pub with my friends the final piece of the jigsaw.

Thoughts of the pub and my friends bring with it the images of Dani, the new barmaid at my local. Fuelled by thoughts of her I smile to myself. Maybe I am finally on the mend and at last I can find the courage to ask Dani out without the fear of rejection tearing me apart. After air drying on my bed releases the final aches form my body, I begin slipping into my clothes. Picking up my shirt reveals a new book, *The Magic Cottage* by James Herbert. Making a mental note to thank Mam for the book I skip back to my bed; all thoughts of going out forgotten, at least for a little while.

My Mam's voice cuts through my reverie:

'Steven, Rossy's on the phone.'

'Ok Mam I'm coming.'

A quick glance at my watch shows 8:30. Ninety minutes lost in the pages of a good book. A rueful smile on my face I leap the stairs two at a time. I immediately hear the laughter at the other end of the line before my mate Rossy speaks:

'Yo! Pretty boy, less of the beautifying and get your arse around here. Poor Danielle is pining for her little boy lost.'

The sound of a slap brings a smirk to my reddening face.

'Give me five minutes and get the bottles in, it must be your turn by now.'

Slamming the phone down before my mate gets the chance to answer, I quickly retrace my steps. In moments I am dressed, coat on and heading out of the door, while shouting a final goodbye to my parents.

The iciness of the night forces my hands further into my pockets and my neck deeper inside my collar. It feels like all of the heat has been sucked from the night. Even this coldest of nights cannot dampen my good mood or the merry skip in my stride however.

Turning the corner at the end of my street brings the gaily lit pub into sight. Pace quickening I can almost taste the ice cold lager I know will be waiting for me. Cutting across the verge instead of following the path, I skirt close to the Old Saxon church surrounded by its own graveyard. The centrepiece of the village, quaint in daylight becomes an eerie, ghostly, monolith as darkness falls. For the first time in all my years living here, I finally see how scary this church becomes when shrouded in darkness. No searchlights that have become common to other churches appeased the midnight hue of night in this little village. Laughing at my own scary thoughts I snuggle deeper into my coat, wishing I had worn my hat and gloves. The temperature plummets yet again. Fervent movement snaps my head back toward the pub, which is briefly obscured in the white plumes of breath escaping my lips. Studying the pub I search for whatever had caught my attention. Seeking an answer my eyes are drawn to the outside lights which seem a little dimmer as if bathed in a coating of oil. Seeing no answer was forthcoming I set off again for the pub.

Upon my first step, the lights outside the pub dim again, closely followed by the entire village. 'What the hell?' I wonder. I struggle for answers, accepting and discarding each one in turn, till only one remains. Power cut imminent. Curiosity growing by the second , I quickly search each part of the village, waiting to see the lights finally flicker and die, followed by the first peals of laughter from the pub. Taking a step forward, my head swinging to and fro I search the village for an answer.

When looking toward the outskirts of the village, it appears although these lights are dim; they are still brighter than the ones around the pub. This being said it still appears that the entire village appears coated in a murky film; making sharp edges ill-defined and almost smoky in appearance. Shadows seem to writhe within the coating that is obscuring the lights throughout the village. Moving from translucent to opaque the nearer my sight travels to the centre; where the old church is supposed to be. Now an almost solid mass of darkness lies over it, obscuring the quaint reminder of Christianity from my sight. Taking a step in retreat I sense rather than see the ridge forming over the church. More shadows pulse toward the ridge and then they appear.

Eyes!

Twin orbs of fathomless ebony staring down toward me. Recoiling in horror, my mind locks my body whilst struggling to process what lies before me. This murky shadow engulfs the whole village, from riverbank to the one road leading in and out of the village. Still held rigid in my own fear, my eyes are drawn into its eyes drawing me forward, hypnotising me, and pulling me toward its centre. Feeling the icy intrusion in its gaze, my mind recoils back to reality, screaming for me to get the hell out of there. My eyes swivel back to the pub, looking at its dimly flickering lights, I take my first step toward sanctuary.

Only thirty yards separate me from salvation. Breaking into a sprint, I head for the one place I know I will find people. Glancing sideways, the houses on the outskirts of the village snap back into normality as this thing, this wraith begins its metamorphism into a new form. Watching in horror, my mind screams a pitiful wail.

Fingers!

My bruised mind has no answers but urges me to slap my feet quicker on the tarmac leading to salvation. More shadows pulse to the smoky fingers of the wraith enabling another metamorphosis.

'My God' is the only answer my tortured mind can muster when the talons begin to take shape.

'For fuck's sake, what the hell is going on?' My mind asks the question but can find no answer.

Looking behind me, my eyes are greeted by the same apparition. Talons already on the move, seeking me out, but these ones are a hell of a lot closer. Heart slamming in my chest, from my efforts, or my fear I don't know, but, the outcome is the same. Knees rising, feet slamming, I re-double my efforts to reach the pub. Racing up the two flights of steps to the pub I rip open the door. Back braced I wait for the talons that would surely rip into my body. Flinging myself inside I breathe a sigh of relief when the door clatters shut behind me.

Staring through the glass panels at my feet I wait for the talons to seep through the glass; knowing in my heart I may have just cost the lives of everyone in the bar. Pulling my knees up till they lie under my chin, I watch and wait. A small wispy tendril breaches the gap and I can only stare in disbelief at the speed of its retreat.

Pulling myself off the floor, I squint in the bright lights hanging over my head. All eyes are on me!

Grasping the offered bottle from Rossy, I swiftly drain two thirds of it in one swallow. Taking a cigarette from my pocket I light it in an attempt to hide my ravaged nerves and shaking hands. Inhaling deeply, I remove my cigarette and quickly finish my lager. Waiting for my next bottle I offer my friends a nervous laugh as explanation for my rather strange entrance.

'Damn bloody laces.'

Slowly night-time in the pub returns to normal and my bruised mind finally resembles something of its former self. Staring from window to window I notice that the wraith has again settled above the church. Its talons shaping and re-shaping like fingers clenching and unclenching into a fist. Centre shifting again, its eyes appear to stare deep into mine. I take a step back under the weight of shivers walking my spine. Turning on my heel I offer my back in a vain hope of forgetting what waits outside for me.

My friends attempt to draw me out but to no avail. Silent, tongue-tied and dejected I slump at the bar, wondering if the village was going to survive this night. After a few strangers had left and made it to their cars intact, one fact was sure; the wraith was waiting for only one person tonight. Maybe I should have said something, but who would have believed me. It appeared that no one else could see it anyway. As the night ticks by, the early leavers run the gauntlet and make it home unscathed.

Last orders ring out!

My friends finish their drinks and shrugging into coats make ready for their short journeys home. Each of my friends live within sight of the pub and watching them leave, I long to open up and tell them what has happened thus keeping them safe. Fear of ridicule, that old thorn in my side, strangles my power of speech and I leave them to the night.

My eyes follow the journey of each and every one of them, my silent prayers a poor excuse for my silence. As each of them enters their own private sanctuary I feel my relief choking me.

One by one the pub empties and alone I stand; a silhouetted prey for the waiting horror outside. Looking at the church our eyes lock, hunter and prey playing a game for my survival. Turning my back again, I slowly drain my final bottle. Shrugging into my coat I spark up a last cigarette and step outside, ready at last to meet my fate. I speak no goodbyes as the door shuts behind me, because like a whippet I am off running into the night.

In the space of two yards my escape ends, when a smoky talon slams into my stomach. If only I had taken a final look, taken the time to look once more through the windows and search the night for my nemesis. Then I would have known it had moved. Draped across the small copse of trees opposite the pub it has laid in wait, probably watching my every move. Hindsight, a bloody curse, for a sack of meat now hangs on a transparent talon, waiting for the horror to begin. None of it matters now; the talon is sinking deeper and is already on the move seeking my heart. Coming out of the night, a second talon sinks into my head freezing my thoughts. Impaled upon the talons I feel myself lifted and dragged forward towards the centre of the wraith. All thoughts of escape are lost in the pain ripping through my body and echoed in my frozen silent screams.

I wait for death.

In its urgent probing of my body I feel the pressure on my head relent a fraction. A final thought escapes from me; my children. Whispered words of sorry send the images of their faces racing through my brain, pushing the pressure burning in my skull back just a little. With a little room to think I take my chance to say goodbye to my children and send a silent message across the night filled with love and apologies. Finally at peace, I am ready to face my own death, filled with the knowledge that my love for them will be a fitting epitaph.

Howling in agony the wraith hurls me to the ground; recoiling from me almost in disgust. Picking myself up from our frozen battlefield, I begin my escape again. Slamming down the steps I somehow keep my balance and hit the grass verge in a full on sprint. Lengthening my stride, I set off on a final run hoping to save my life. Maybe just maybe I can make this and for the first time since leaving my home I dare to feel hope. I was free, something had hurt it and I now knew that it wasn't the light, but the heat that had caused the wraith's disgust in me. My love for my children, the heat of human kindness, love for a fellow person, all these had prevented the wraith from following me into the pub and from killing me as I left.

I have only one chance left, a small glimmer of hope to end this night alive and I am ready to put it into play. A few yards from home I stop, my chest heaving, head hung low and waiting. The first talon smokes through my arm. Frozen pain erupts nauseating me at this fresh assault. Arm hanging useless I still wait. A second talon ghosts through the top of my thigh freezing me to the spot. Bringing its head level with mine the wraith begins again violating my body with more of its noxious self.

'Come on you bastard,' I scream.

The wraith is all too willing. Forcing more of itself inside me, it begins filling my every cell and overloading me till I believe I may explode. Now it's my turn. Opening my mind I parade the images of my children; a slideshow of love, warmth and understanding. The unconditional love of a Father, raw and honest, one of the most powerful emotions one can hold. As one slideshow finishes another starts, friendship, first loves, laughs and smiles, I parade them all. Recoiling again in its own agony, the wraith retreats into itself, gradually diminishing in size until only its eyes remain in the trees of the graveyard.

Turning my back I walk the few yards to my door and slip quietly into my home. Pain is a powerful negative emotion and tonight I guess I saw just how powerful. Taking my phone from my pocket, I slowly key in a number and allow a sigh to escape me. Listening to her voice on the other end of the line, I dare to smile.

DANCE OF DEATH

JOSH CHRISTIAN

I wasn't drunk. Well… maybe somewhat. On the surface, that night seemed at first to be just like any other, but it was barely midnight; there was time yet.

Like a lost and downtrodden fool I wandered through the Everglades, enjoying the bright moonlight and gazing up at the stars. It was a beautiful night, weather-wise; a cloudless sky; the air, warm and still. The world was at peace. Then there was me. Propped up against a lamppost in my undersized shoes, I hung on to stop myself falling into the abyss of the gutter, in which rancid water was bubbling up through the grate. In my arms I cradled a half-empty bottle of gin, and I was glaring at my reflection in a dime-store window. Hair bedraggled and matted, eyes bagged and bloodshot, clothes soiled and stained; I looked a grotesque example of a human being. The world was far too busy to care about a divorced, piss-stained, failed artist. The world was too busy to care about the troubles of such people, yet troubles I had: a bum job that paid worse than shit, and a family who didn't want to know. I was in a hole, a hole from which no level of alcoholism could help me escape. It had been all too easy to end up in this state, yet it was damn near impossible to drag myself out. What I needed was a spark, something to change my life for the better, to help me make something of myself, as my parents so often used to claim was as unlikely as me ever selling a sketch. Bowing my head and revelling in self-pity, I trudged on through the deserted streets, not knowing where I was heading; like a blind man in an empty room.

I had walked these streets for years, but still they were alien to me. Florida was no Nevada, but there was work in Florida, and no haunting nightmares, no cursed memories hiding round the corners, no ghosts of the past waiting to leap out when I least expected it. Honestly, I thought, death would be preferable. Still, I wandered on, not aware of a presence so near to me, watching my every move.

Acting like a sniffer dog searching for a cold trail, I rounded a bend and found myself in the main boulevard of town, a blank mass of glass and concrete. The street was silent, bathed in the steely grey of early summer moonlight. Before long this place would be full to overflowing, cars and buses roaring past, shoppers bustling from store to store gossiping, thinking, living. But for now, all was still and quiet. The creak of an advertising board sounded up ahead, and glancing blearily towards it, my gaze was drawn to a particularly run-down store, named 'Stanton Levey Taxidermy'. To my knowledge, the place hadn't been open for business for years; always the sign on the door read 'closed'.

The shop-front was cluttered with out of date religious flyers and church event advertisements, and on a pedestal behind the glass stood a dusty old stuffed goat, its fiery glass eyes forever watching the world go by. The store had a recessed entrance, which was shrouded in shadow, seemingly immune to the light of the moon. That would be the perfect place for an attacker to hide. In fact, *was* there someone there? It was far too dark to tell for sure, but I could vaguely make out the figure of a... something. Whatever it was, it was tall, hulking, menacing.

Fear began to tickle my insides, and I made to turn back. But I saw, with a rush of panic and alarm, the figure move into the open. It wore a cloak draped over its frame, and a cowl was pulled low over its head. It moved into the middle of the sidewalk, and stood deathly still, facing me. Panic mingled with fear, and fear mixed with dread, as the figure stood, as still as a headstone, washing me in blind terror. What it was, I do not know, but I could guess, and what I envisioned still haunts me to this day.

The hallucination started walking, slowly, purposefully, towards the corner on which I stood; towards me. I fell to my knees, and let my half-empty bottle of gin hit the floor with a hollow clunk.

I watched, frozen with fear, as the figure approached. A chill, a deathly chill, not that of a summer's evening, not of this world, froze my lungs, rendering me speechless. Even so, had I been able to, I wouldn't have screamed; I was frozen, paralyzed. The evil apparition approached, stopped, not two feet away, and bent its cowl-covered face, arching its back as if bending for a kiss. A hand, a rotten, scabbed, maggot infested hand was drawn out from beneath the folds of the cloak. A forefinger was extended. It moved towards my helpless, immobile body. Time slowed, the stars twinkled, and my heart beat. The gangrenous finger was placed upon my forehead.

There was no pain. There was nothing. For a length of time unfathomable to living men, there was nothing. The darkness eventually started to take me, and I let it, I even welcomed it, and for the first time in my life, I wished for death.

The darkness engulfed me, and I knew that I was dead. There was nothing. So this was it? This was death? It wasn't so bad, this nothingness. But wait, there had to be something; I was thinking, and, yes, I was seeing: the stars had fallen to earth; they were dancing before my eyes, a beautiful, sparkling dance of life. But was this earth? Was this life? I doubted it.

Within moments the stars had begun to fade, to be replaced by a vast expanse of blackness. I had heard tales of death being like a tunnel of darkness leading towards a bright light. A tunnel there was not, but a light there most certainly was. A bright light - that of a gigantic flame - swam before my eyes, about one-hundred paces away. I started towards it, walking through the unknown realm of darkness with resigned conviction. If this was heaven, I didn't think much of it; however, if it was something else...

Upon drawing near, I saw that I was not looking at any mundane flame, but at a ring of fire, no less than a hundred feet in diameter, flames dancing far above me. This was an unholy place. I stood in front of it, a sense of awe taking the place of any fear I had experienced. The heat of the fire was unnerving, it was not hot, nor was it cold. It was, unmistakably, welcoming. I wondered what to do, should I step through and beyond, or am I meant to wait?

Despite the comforting warmth of the fire, I dared not cross through, dared not take the final step. It was then that I saw, through the flames, something most definitely unholy. Figures, dozens, if not hundreds, were gathered within the circle of fire. Transfixed, I watched as they swayed peacefully, unaware of my presence, a sense of serenity becoming almost palpable. It was not long until one approached. It was summoning me over to join them. As if time had stood still, I was numb with fear but still, I wanted to go. Into the circle of fire I followed him; and into the middle I was led. The blaze of the fire did not hurt me, as I walked onto the coals.

The figures, grotesque distortions of human beings, stood still and watched my approach, eager expressions on their faces. They were the embodiment of evil. They were, most assuredly, dead, yet they moved with grace; solid grace, not unlike that of a ballet dancer. Their mutilated faces were partly covered with masks, yet this did not lessen the grotesquery of the sight. The masks were fashioned from bones; human skulls adorned with miniscule bones and cartilage. The Dead wore costumes, made from what was unmistakably, flayed, human skin. The skins of men, women, and children, swam morbidly before my eyes, draped over the shoulders of the abominations before me; the sight caused me to retch.

Not content with the bones and skin of the newly deceased, the Dead wore necklaces of teeth, earrings suspended with eyes, and bracelets of fingernails. The result was ghastly, sickening, and awe-inspiring. I felt I was in a trance, as if my spirit had been lifted from me, and I could not help but watch, as they began the Dance of Death.

Music, callous and evil, began to reverberate around the ring of fire. A group of figures, sitting aside, around the perimeter of the circle, had in front of them the most bizarre and awful assortment of instruments I had ever seen. Drums, fashioned from skulls, were being played; the Dead thumping craniums, resulting in a deathly rhythmic beating; violas strung with the heartstrings of men were shrieking sickeningly; and bassoons carved from the bones of the damned, hummed evocatively, capable of shaking the very foundations of the soul.

The Dead were dancing, slowly, hypnotically, their contorted limbs moving with an unnatural grace. Their eyes were closed, as if in silent revelry, lost in the ghastly music, their skin costumes swaying rhythmically. The cacophonous music smothering my ears, I stood, looking on with a potent sense of revulsion, and, disturbingly, intrigue. The Dead were moving with a grace not becoming of their twisted bodies, but were bowing, turning and sweeping in gracious arcs. Before I realised I was doing so, I was dancing with them. I felt like a puppet having its strings twitched by some unseen puppeteer; yet I knew I was in control. Had I wished to stop dancing at that moment, I feel I would have been able to, but for the moment, I let myself get lost within the music, which had increased in tempo.

Skulls were drummed harder, faster; viola strings bowed with increased pitch and rigour; bassoons blown to their full capacity. The sound was awful. The dancing had turned wild. The mangled bodies of the Dead were whirling through the air, spinning frantically, tearing around the circle, creating a blur of flesh, bone and blood. I danced, and I pranced, and I sang with them, all had death in their eyes. The lifeless figures, they were undead, all of them... they had ascended from Hell.

The dance had become frenzied. Undead bodies were hurling themselves against one another, crashing into anything that stood in their way. The music had turned frantic. The Dead whirled hysterically, and as they did so, the fires roared, and they were dancing too, flickering wildly and flashing fitfully, blasting out an unworldly heat. I was knocked to my knees, colliding with what should have been floor. But the floor was covered with water, water that was red; dyed by the blood of the dead.

Revulsion and dread burst through me as realisation set in; a deep, sticky, rancid torrent of blood was spreading, not from me, as I had first feared, but it was bubbling out from under me, from the abyss. The dancing Dead splashed through the pool, showering my crumpled form with the blood of countless victims, victims claimed over millennia.

Victims like me?

The music ringing painfully, the Dead dancing wickedly, the fire burning brilliantly, a figure began to rise from the centre of the circle. Through the bubbling blood, and into the centre of the thrashing Dead, the Master had risen. A mass of tangled muscle, skin, and bone, topped with the unmistakable mutilated head of a goat; Hell embodied. Nine feet tall, doused in the blood of the dead, the Beast towered above his servants, who were slamming themselves to the floor, bowing, screaming, and weeping in fevered adulation. They raised and lowered their masked faces into the mass of blood, apparently bathing in the blood of Hell's children; the red soup washed down their faces, mixed with their tears, and formed tacky goo which clung to their faces.

Petrified beyond belief, my eyes were held by the Master, with eyes that burned more fiercely than the circle of fire. I hadn't met the maker, I had met the destroyer. The Beast looked away, extended his arms, and acknowledged the exultation of his dancing Dead. The time had come to unite me with my eternal soul, the Master was about to claim his next victim of death. At that moment my spirit came back down to me, I didn't know if I was alive or dead.

This was my fate; to forever protect the first circle of Hell, to welcome the endless torrent of damned souls and escort them to their eternal doom. But I wasn't ready. I wanted to live. If this was my fate then I wanted to go back, to live my life as I should have lived it. I had been looking for a spark, this was it. I turned; the Dead had taken their attention away from me. When He took His gaze from me was the moment that I fled. I ran like hell, faster than the wind. I ran through the ring of fire, feeling skin instantly vaporising from my bones, but still I ran. There was no pursuit; no damned creatures dragging me down into the abyss, so still I ran, until I hit something immovably solid.

I had slammed back to earth. There was no pain. I wasn't drunk. I was buzzing with shock, my ears were still ringing, and my breath was still heaving. Yet I was back, undoubtedly back. I could feel the cold of the sidewalk against my face. My knees were stinging, grazed from when I had fallen and the cramping of my toes in my too-small shoes throbbed.

Not quite daring to believe I was free, I pushed myself up, eyes snapping open. Yes, I was alive, I could see; I was back. There were the moon and the stars; there were the glass fronted stores; and there was my half-full bottle of gin. I was on my feet, filling my lungs with crisp air that felt like soup. Life flickered through me, like a newly kindled flame, and awareness of what I had just escaped burned itself into my soul. I was alive, and I would keep it that way.

I looked left and right, there was no sign of the cloaked figure. I looked down at myself; there was no trace of blood upon my shirt. Had it been real? Oh yes, it had been real; the fact that your body doesn't come with you does not prevent something being real. I had had a taste of what awaited my soul should I continue on this road of wasting and wandering; that was what could be… this is what is; make the most of it while it lasts.

To this day I guess I'll never know just why they let me go; but I'll never go dancing any more until I dance with the Dead.

GH3

CAITLIN WILSON

Rain fell about the house, like the scrabbling of mice behind walls, Timothy ducked into his study, locking the door behind him and turning on the gas lamps to their full burn. He ran his hands through his hair, despite being in his late twenties it was already flecked with grey; a common affliction of the males of the Braithwaite family. Timothy crossed the room and sat at the large desk, a letter explaining the previous occupancy of the manor house lay open before him.

His late uncle, Carlton Braithwaite, had purchased the Manor House a few months after its previous occupant, a Doctor Charles Jaloux, had been found hanging in the scullery. Charles' Father was French and had moved to England after marrying an Englishwoman; together the Jaloux's had purchased the manor, raised their son and then willed it to him and his wife Elizabeth after they died. Life was perfect at the Manor House, until Elizabeth vanished one cold, winter morning. The household staff and local villagers swapped stories of how she had ran off with her lover. After a fortnight of her absence, Charles never spoke of her again.

Feeling suddenly uneasy Timothy turned sharply, nearly upsetting the inkpots on the desk but finding only the portrait of his Uncle staring back at him. Feeling rather foolish, and somewhat unnerved by the storm outside, he pulled forward the stack of unanswered correspondents and set to work.

The house that Timothy resided in had briefly belonged to his late Uncle, and was left to him in Carlton's will. Carlton's body had been found in the corridor housing the family portraits. The coroner reported the cause of death as heart failure, although the look of horror frozen across the contours of his face suggested that something had scared him so badly that his heart had given out under the strain.

Several minutes later, as Timothy was responding to the first of his correspondents, there was a loud, long, echoing crash from somewhere on the upper floor. Timothy was startled to his feet; he knew he was alone in the house as no staff were due to arrive yet. He gathered a handful of candles from one of the desk draws and fixed them into the gilt candelabrum that stood on a small table. Lightning flashed across the windows as he lit the candles.

Curious to find the cause of the disturbance, Timothy unlocked the door and made his way toward the grand staircase, leaving the gas lamps glowing; the study seemed rather merry in contrast to the unfamiliar, dark corridors of the manor.
 He pulled at the ties of his dressing gown. A chill had risen from the floor beneath his bare feet. Timothy was glad of the warmth from the candles as the Manor House had cooled significantly since the storm had moved in.

His footsteps were stifled by the crimson carpets laid on the staircase. He caught his reflection in the large window. As he passed by, a low boom of thunder rolled around Braithwaite Manor. Timothy leant forward to inspect his appearance by candle light. He frowned, his hair was in need of cutting; in a sweeping motion he brushed back the fallen strands of hair. A flash of lightning lit up the moor outside almost simultaneously. A face, which was not his own, glared back at Timothy in the fleeting illumination. He gave a yell and leapt away from the window as if he had been struck by the lightning itself. The face had been long, gaunt and almost yellow in hue, with impossibly wide, black eyes as if its pupils had been blown fully open; its mouth twisted into such a horrid snarl that it exposed all of its disgusting teeth.

The pounding in his chest at last subsiding, Timothy gingerly stepped forward, unable to stop the muscle twitching in his thigh as he readied himself to jump back if necessary. Seconds passed, but in the candle light there was no sign of the apparition, nor of anything else; just his reflection staring cautiously back at him.

'Good Lord', Timothy thought, 'am I hallucinating? Am I going mad?'

He held his hand to his forehead; warm but not feverishly so. He backed away from the window and continued up the stairs, unable to bring himself to look back.

Timothy searched the upper floor methodically, looking into each room he came to, but nothing seemed out of place; each of the white sheets, acting as dust collectors over his uncle's belongings, were still.
'I don't understand,' Timothy said aloud to a porcelain bust, 'What could have made that noise? And what the devil was that ghastly thing at the window, if it was ever there at all?'

He shuddered as the thunder trolled over the house and he left the room to continue his search.

The shadows cast from the candles flickered eerily over the paintings framed upon the walls. Timothy hadn't bothered looking at them in any great detail before he had moved in but looking at them now he could see that while some of them were landscapes, the majority were portraits.

Leaning closer to the canvases in the light of the candles, he was able to pick out the familiar features in the haughty faces. He slowly progressed down the corridor, seeing the same nose or bow-shaped lips in some of the portraits. It wasn't until he found himself looking into the painted eyes of his Grandfather that he realised the paintings were of his ancestors. He doubled back over quite a few generations and traced the male grey hair back to a portrait near the top of the corridor. It was a tall, thin man from whom Timothy seemed to have inherited his upturned nose. The name plate on the frame read 'Douglas Adam Braithwaite'. Underneath was his birth and death date. Timothy found that he was standing before his great-great-great-great-great Grandfather.

A further rumble of thunder reminded him of the task in hand; with a nervous glance toward the nearest window he continued up the hall to find the source of the disturbance.

Timothy brushed his fingers along the wall, careful to skim over the frames rather than the canvases. The wind had picked up again outside, whistling around the Manor House in unnaturally pitched tones. The candles in the candelabrum began to waver violently, casting distorted shadows across the family paintings.

Timothy raised his dusty hand away from the wall to protect the dancing flames from the sudden draught. He looked wildly around for the source of the breeze, but instead he made out a large, rectangular object stretched out on the floor of the adjoining corridor. He ducked out of the draught and into the hall. He lowered his hand and light spilled out from behind it, revealing the back of an old canvas; from which the wire had become detached loosening it from the wall.

Timothy set the candelabrum down close to the wall to avoid any more rogue draughts. Now with both hands free, he grasped the frame and heaved it upright, propping it against the wall from which it had fallen. It was no mean feat; the painting was the same size as the bedroom doors. Before he could reach for the candles another shock of lightning lit up the hallway. Timothy recoiled and made to throw his arm across his face, expecting the vile creature from the window to leap out of the painting at him. He laughed nervously as he lowered his arm and took up the candelabrum again, stepping back to admire the painting in full view.

It was a landscape of the moor from the front of the manor. The artist had captured the barrenness of the land in extraordinary detail.   Timothy checked the bottom corner and found it was dated that very year.

'Uncle Carlton must have had this commissioned when he first moved here,' Timothy's voice carried down the empty halls.

He studied the painting, admiring how the candle light picked out the lilac in the purple moor heather. It wasn't until he held the candelabrum to the wall brackets that he noticed what the painting had been hiding; the stonework beneath the painting was different from that surrounding it. Timothy doubted he would have even noticed it if the painting hadn't fallen down.

'How curious; there must have been a doorway here at some point. I wonder why it was bricked up. Perhaps Uncle wrote of it in one of his diaries.'

Timothy rapped his knuckles along the stretch of new stone as he turned and made his way towards the library.

The darkness and silence of the library was suffocating. Timothy stumbled over the various rugs and boxes until he found the chest containing Carlton Braithwaite's journals. It didn't take long to find the journal coinciding with his uncle's purchase of the house and flicked to its later entries. Timothy felt a small ache as he saw that it was written the day before his uncle died; the final entry of his uncle's life. He skimmed down the paragraphs, promising himself that he'd read it in detail at a later date. Finally he came across a section referring to the wall itself.

It read:

I arrived home yesterday to find that the painting of the moor I requested had been completed and delivered. Thomas and Joseph of the household staff have hung it perfectly. No one would ever guess the blemish hidden beneath it. Whilst they were attaching the painting to its brackets, they noticed that both of the brackets and the surrounding bricks were loose; I'll have to make a note for someone to send word to the village tomorrow.

There was a strange occurrence during the night. I have lived in the manor for several weeks now but this was the first I have experienced. I would swear that I was awoken by a woman crying down the corridor where the new painting hangs. However, excluding Mrs Hope who assures me it was not her, there are no women in this household. There was nothing there when I went to investigate. It may have been nonsense but I felt as if there had been some sort of presence; the corridor itself was significantly cooler than the one previous.

    Timothy closed the journal and sat back in the covered armchair. The candelabrum stood on the mantle of the empty fireplace, reflecting gently in the mirror above the stonework. The glass ceiling above him revealed the storm clouds outside; purple, like the spring heather in the painting. For a brief moment there was silence, no wolf-like wind howled, not a floorboard creaked as the house settled. Timothy stood up, the diary held loosely in one hand; his mouth fell open as he admired the swirling, deep violet clouds as they mixed with the amethyst coils in the veiled moonlight.

    A deep rumble of thunder and a stark flash of lightning illuminated the library. Timothy caught sight of the room behind him in the mirror. His jaw fell open again, not in admiration but in horror. As clear as day in the lingering light, Timothy saw the shelves from the great bookcases torn from their confines. The upholstery was uncovered: long scars revealing the stuffing like some obscene fluid from a wound; the wooden skeleton showing through like bone puncturing through skin. Mounds of books lay defiled, covers ripped away from their spines; some plummeted from the higher shelves like grim birds with broken wings, while musty pages rained down, chasing each other in a macabre dance. The figure from the window stood a few metres behind him, its mouth twisted into a silent roar, unexplainable fury glaring from the deep pits of its eyes; a vivid purple bruise hung around its sinewy neck. As the light faded, its arm shot up to grab at Timothy. Plunged into darkness, Timothy snatched up the candelabrum and spun on his heels; he staggered forward but was met by nothing. The library was empty and very much intact as it had been when he first entered.

    Timothy backed out of the library, swinging the candles in the empty darkness; he hurried back to the stairs to follow through on the only thing that made sense to him. He was going to find out what was behind that wall.

    He started with the wall brackets. Once those had been wriggled out, the newer brickwork around them came out easily; for the ones that couldn't be pulled away by hand Timothy used the iron brackets to hammer and chip at the sealing mortar between the stones.

    He ignored the rain pounding on the windows and carried on working. With a grunt Timothy forced a large slab from the wall and retched. A putrid stench flowed from the alcove behind the stonework, Timothy gagged, tasting whatever was behind the wall at the back of his mouth. He couldn't stop himself, a grotesque curiosity took over and adrenaline flooded his limbs. Sweat was beaded on his brow rolling down his neck and back, absorbed by the dressing gown that was now keeping him overly warm.

    The last two feet of stone came away together; the smell so disgusting that Timothy covered his nose with the damp collar of his dressing gown as the candle light swept into the alcove. He stood in shock when he saw what had been bricked up, then wrenched the fabric away from his face and fell to his knees vomiting violently.

    He wiped his mouth weakly on his sleeve. The rotten remains of a corpse lay before him. The flesh had all but deteriorated, but still clung to the protruding bone. Somewhere in the overwhelming sickness and haze of revulsion Timothy noted that it

had once been a woman. Her dress was bloody and what was left of her hair lay knotted around her shoulders. Timothy sat opposite her; his mind overflowing with fear, questions and uncertainty. When the corpse's head dropped, its empty sockets bore straight into Timothy's horrified eyes. Then slowly, the fleshless jaw opened.
'Run,' The skeleton hissed. 'He'll be here soon. Run.'

Timothy launched himself to his feet, colliding into the wall behind him and knocking several paintings to the floor. As they clattered and clashed around him, the corpse twitched and slowly pulled herself up.
'Go. I'll hold him off. Run.'

What was left of her tongue protruded absurdly as she spoke. Timothy sank against the wall; it was too much, his body shivered violently as he tried to squirm away from the corpse.

'This isn't possible. How? Wh-what?'

Timothy's limbs seemed to find strength from his own voice. He made a desperate leap for the candelabrum and swung it between them. The corpse lifted her hands, the fleshy tips of her fingers were missing and the bone was worn down.

'If you do not wish to suffer as your Uncle and I did, then you will leave now.'

Before Timothy could answer the paintings at the bottom of the hall were ripped from the walls by an invisible force and hurled up the corridor toward him.

Not entirely sure why, Timothy breathed a ragged 'thank you' to the corpse woman before bolting down the corridor, his dressing gown undulating behind him.

He didn't stop, not even to draw breath; he hurtled down the staircase, past the gas lamp lit study throwing himself against the large, oak front door. A woman's scream came from upstairs just as Timothy's hand found the key in the lock; he wrenched the door open and fled into the night.

SMILE

CHLOE CHARLTON

They stood, their bodies still and rigid, my eyes drawn to their identical, disfigured faces. Many were newly cut, stitches sticking out, blood smeared, faces forced into smiles. But their eyes were cold. Their eyes were dead.

And then she stepped forward, clutching the knife, the knuckles of her left hand white and prominent. The corners of her lips quirked upwards, pushing the jagged scars up so that her face became a sickening caricature of a smile.

'Come on. It's your turn.'

I took a step backward, as she raised the knife.

In the beginning, it was just a normal day.
I stood in front of the mirror, staring at the reflection of my pale, plain face. My hair was combed neatly and pushed back behind my ears, which I had always thought stuck out a little too much. My feet in their shiny new shoes were pressed together, and my skinny knees were bent at awkward angles. I sighed.

'Smile!' said my Mother, coming up behind me with a grin spreading from ear to ear. 'You look fine.'

I forced a smile. Today was my first day back at school. I was invisible there, wandering the corridors like a ghost, with only one real friend by my side. But I did what I always did; I picked up my bag and left the house.

They were crammed into the corridors, flitting around and talking in unison so that all I could hear was one loud, flat drone. They were like worker bees, constantly in motion, their eyes shining and their mouths open wide as they relayed their stories of the summer whispering the newest gossip with hushed giggles and accusing glances. At our school, there weren't lots of separate cliques. It was just them, and everybody else.
'Melissa!'

The cry came from my right, and before I had a chance to blink, I felt the air being crushed out of my lungs as a pair of arms were wrapped tightly around me.

'Hi, Lucy.'

My best friend. With her round face, springy red curls and bright eyes, I could always count on her. She was always there, always had been, and always would be.

'Have you seen the new girl? I heard some people talking about her, apparently she's really mysterious. Nobody knows where she moved from. She has a scar or something.'

I shook my head. 'No, I haven't seen her, but I guess I will. The school isn't that big.'

I saw her a few hours later, as I was heading to my locker.
She was pushing her way through the crowd; all I could see was a sheet of dark blonde hair and a long black coat. But then they noticed her, they stopped talking, and she stopped pushing through. They began to move aside, creating a path for her. Their eyes were wide, their mouths parted. I couldn't tell if they were enchanted or appalled by the sight of her. Either way, she had a bigger effect on them than anyone I'd ever seen walking down that corridor. Frowning, I found a place to squeeze in, and at that moment, she caught my eye. She looked at me, and I looked at her, and I saw her face.

She had two scars, long, thin and jagged, beginning at the edges of her lips and reaching up to the top of her cheeks. I had the feeling that they had been made long ago, yet somehow they looked new, as though the skin would simply break open again at any moment, spilling blood and opening a gaping hole in her face. They were a deep red, matching the colour of her lips and standing out against her pale skin, stretching across her high cheekbones to create the image of a sinister, permanent smile. Her eyes were dark, but bright, as though black beetles had nested inside her empty eye sockets. She reminded me of a skeleton. She looked like death.

She looked right at me, and she smiled.

I can't explain what happened then. Something shifted in me, or maybe the world changed around me. Dark shadows seemed to emerge from corners and from behind tall, looming objects to swoop around me and hug me tight, wrapping me up in an icy blanket.

But then there came the bell, and I was pulled back into reality. It sounded more like a whistle, high and shrill, piercing my skull, bouncing off my eardrums like a tiny bullet. With a blink, she had turned and continued walking, along with the rest of them. I watched the back of her sand-coloured head, the swish of her long coat, until she was gone.

A cold, clammy feeling washed over me then. I couldn't move, could barely breathe. I felt sick to the stomach, weak, dizzy.

I leaned against the wall, reaching out behind me for support feeling the cool, flaking paint beneath my fingertips. I closed my eyes tight, and then her disfigured face, smiling as wide as a skeleton.

'Liss?'

I opened my eyes. Lucy. She gazed at me, green eyes round and wide.
'Are you okay?'

I nodded and stood straighter, pulling my hand away from the wall; my fingers were clammy, sticky, and I knew they would have left damp prints on the paint.

'I'm fine, I just felt a little dizzy,' I smiled, hoping it was convincing. 'We'd better go to history.'

I looked straight ahead of me as I walked, but I could feel Lucy throwing several concerned glances my way. I was fine. The girl hadn't done anything to me, and she probably didn't intend to either. I suddenly felt horribly guilty, judgmental, cruel. I was acting like the girls I hated, judging someone because of their appearance, fearing something that she was probably really insecure about. I decided that the next time I saw her I would smile, or find a compliment to give her. She must have been lonely, if everyone had that reaction to her.

But the next day, everything had already started to change.

They adored her. Whenever I saw her, in lessons, in the hallways, outside, she was always surrounded by a group of girls, boys, admirers. It wasn't always the same people. There were us, and Them. We were the invisible. They were the social, the well known, the beautiful. And They worshipped her.

Her name was Elizabeth, and she became the most popular girl in school. I even caught Lucy gazing at her from afar, watching her talking and laughing with the others. I didn't understand it. I didn't know what they saw in her, but then I felt guilty for thinking that. If they could be so accepting of somebody who did not fit their idea of beautiful, then it had to be the start of something good.

I was so horribly wrong about that.

One weekend, there had been a party, and all of them had gone. I stayed at home as usual, doing schoolwork and reading. Monday morning was full of chatter, excited talk of the things that they had done at the party. I drifted around, catching bits of gossip here and there, until I noticed something that made me stop still and drop the books that I was carrying. A chill rushed through me, and I felt sick, so sick. A small group of girls were huddled around Elizabeth, laughing. And they all had her scars. Their faces had been cut, and they were swollen and pink, the deep cuts in their cheeks kept closed with clumsy, messy-looking stitches. It looked agonizing, but they didn't even show a single sign of being in pain. Instead, they just smiled.

The worst part about it was that nobody else seemed to see how horrible it was. Nobody else was staring at them in revulsion, just the same admiration of Elizabeth, and jealousy of the girls that were close to her. I stumbled into a nearby bathroom and threw up my breakfast.

There was somebody who noticed. Somebody who I made eye contact with during my English lesson, and we shared the terror in our glances. It was the teacher, Mr Sander. A group of six of them, four of whom now had their faces cut, came into the classroom late on Wednesday afternoon, laughing and talking loudly, while the rest of us sat silently, glancing at Mr Sander to see how he would react. None of the teachers had spoken up about it yet, though I had seen some of them whispering to each other in doorways, casting worried glances at the scarred students. I didn't understand why they didn't say anything to them. I didn't understand anything; nothing made sense, nothing was right. But Mr Sander spoke up.

'There is an issue that I feel I have to address,' he began, and they looked up and stared at him. 'I understand peer pressure, and what it's like for teenagers, believe me. I was one too once, even though that's hard to believe.'

They stared.

'But this is going too far. It's getting out of hand. It is disgusting how far some people are willing to go to be popular. The staff are getting very worried about this new trend and I'm certain that your parents must be horrified as well. Something will be done about this. It can't go on.'

They stared, and then they looked at each other, and then they smiled.

The next day, Mr Sander showed up to class late. The group from the day before were unusually quiet as they sat in their seats, but occasionally they whispered to each other and broke out in giggles. I knew they had done something. Their stares looked so sinister, their glances so calculating.

The moment Mr Sander finally showed up was the moment that I was sure that there was something supernatural happening at the school; something that went past the normal extreme actions of teenagers. His face was cut. Pinpricks of blood were squeezing their way out past a loose stitch in his right cheek, and he looked right at them and he smiled. They laughed. One of them stood up, a boy with close-cropped dark hair.

'Mr Sander, we're leaving, we don't want to do the stupid test.'

Mr Sander nodded. 'That's fine, John. You go and have fun!'

It all came from Elizabeth. It must be some kind of mind-control, compulsion, brainwashing. They were like a cult, and now they were taking the teachers too.

It just kept getting worse. More and more kids started showing up to school with scarred faces and careless attitudes, but nothing was more horrifying than what I witnessed the following Tuesday afternoon.

Elizabeth was holding a large, jagged knife, and she was laughing at Lucy, while our other old friend Grace stood beside her with a wad of tissues pressed against her face. Blood was soaking through them quickly, and she had tears in her eyes. I stood around a corner, watching.
'Please, Lizzie, let me in. You cut Grace, it would be just as easy to have me too, I promise I'll be a lot of fun!'

'I offered it to you the first day we met, Lucy, and you turned me down. You didn't want to be popular. So now you never will be.'

Lucy shook her head, rubbed at her eyes, and then ran. I stayed where I was, terrified of being noticed, until Elizabeth and Grace had left. Then I walked in the direction Lucy had run, glancing in every room I passed. Then I heard her. She was crying loudly, occasionally gasping and shouting out. The noise was coming from the girl's bathroom. As soon as I walked in, I regretted ever coming back to school after that first day I saw Elizabeth. My best friend was sitting on the floor, a small but sharp craft knife in her shaking hand, and there was blood everywhere. Half of one cheek was cut open, revealing a row of teeth, the blood spilling out onto her shirt; tears pouring down her face. I had never been so terrified, so sick, so sad.

'Am I beautiful yet, Liss?' She sobbed, staring into my eyes. 'Am I good enough yet?'

I backed away, and ran as fast as I could.

And then I was there, in the hallway, surrounded by identical smiles.

'Come on. It's your turn.'

I took a step backward, as she raised the knife.

'No! You'll never take me! I don't want to be like you!'

'Exactly. You're the only person who didn't want in. Why? Who wouldn't want to be popular? Who wouldn't want to be adored?'

I shook my head. 'No. I don't! I don't want it!'

She lunged at me. My head hit the floor hard, and I almost blacked out, my vision blurry. But I had to stay awake. I had to stay me.
   But the knife was already pressed against my cheek, digging in, drawing blood. I screamed, and with a sudden burst of strength, I grabbed her wrist and twisted. It was as cold as ice, and she didn't seem to feel it, but she dropped the knife. I picked it up before she could comprehend what was happening. My heart was thudding, my head felt light, but I knew I had to do this. I had to, nobody else would.
   I thrust my arm at her, and sank the knife right into her middle, slashing through the skin. Or I would have, if there had been skin to cut into. As soon as the knife made contact with Elizabeth, she vanished.
And all around me, teenagers started to cry, to clutch at their faces, to gaze into mirrors and scream.

It took a long time for everything to go back to normal. Nobody could understand what had happened to them, or why. But the popular and beautiful were no more. It was no longer us and Them. They were disfigured, and every one of us was alone.

One day, Lucy came to me. We hadn't spoken since it had happened. She passed a piece of paper to me, and then walked away soundlessly. I looked at the paper, and realised it was a newspaper article from thirty years ago. I began to read.

I stared at the article, and found myself blinking rapidly in an attempt to stop the tears from spilling down my cheeks, threatening to smudge the ink. The words became just as blurry, however, with each horrid sentence that I read. Elizabeth had been bullied, so badly that the word tortured may be more appropriate, and then one day she had been snatched while walking home late one night and dragged back into the abandoned school, where she had been mutilated and eventually, after hours of relentless torment, she had been killed. I gazed at her photograph; without the grotesque scarring, she looked young, fresh-faced and innocent. I supposed that all she had ever wanted was to be one of the popular kids. Finally, she got her wish. I crumpled up the paper in my hands and got to my feet, wiping at my eyes with the back of my hand as I dropped the article and began to walk away. But the image remained as though it had been burned into my mind.

I could still see the hint of a twinkle in her eyes, and the ghost of a smile curving up the corners of her mouth.

Us

Caitlin Wilson

You just walked in one day
and woke us up
You left footprints in our dust
disturbed the spiders from their webs
Why did you come here?
We are curious

You opened our curtains
and light broke in
Ray upon ray
Beaming
Golden
We stood in its wake after you left
hoping to feel the warmth
But we couldn't anything

You kept coming back
and we didn't mind as you tidied us away
We followed you
as you swept away the dust
varnished our stairs
took away our paintings
We left when you killed the spiders
We didn't like that
But you pulled down the curtains
and we watched the sun set

One night you set a fire in the hearth
and we told you our stories
it didn't matter that you didn't listen
it was nice to have someone to talk to since you killed the spiders

Then the day came when you took away the last of our furniture
We don't think you knew it had outlived monarchs

and we were sad to see it broken outside
for the first time
We wanted the curtains back

Then we were angry
Venomously
When you brought her to stay with us
We made the floorboards ache and groan
We shook the windows in the fixings
Slammed doors and held them shut
We burst our pipes and screamed at night
We were happy when she ran away

but you ran after her
and left us
Why?
you cleaned us and listened to our stories
we even forgave you for the spiders
didn't you love us?

THE MAGDALENE ASYLUM

CONOR O'DONOVAN

'Not even the rats will go there', warned the rough, haggard ferryman, 'and I'll certainly not stay on this damned isle'.

It was a hopeless situation. She'd paid the rough-spoken sailor a small fortune just to take her as far as the shore. It would be useless to try to convince him to stay. This would leave her vulnerable and stranded but she could know no peace until her task on the island was complete, and so she sent him on his way back to the safety of the mainland. The young gypsy steadily ascended the steep jagged rocks that surrounded the islands circumference. The spray of the waves berating against the rock helped their silvery white outline become more visible, to the point where even in the desolate night she could discern them, just enough to make out her footing. Her keen senses struggled to adjust. It seemed they were under attack from the island, the dark of the night, the roaring waves and the numbing cold from the water, a cold that was intensified under the clear October sky. As she transcended from rock to grassy earth the sound of the waves faded into the background. Her destination loomed into focus and as it did, the winds around her died. The island off the Irish coast was largely uninhabited and as she came nearer what was once the Magdalene Asylum at the islands centre, no crickets chirped nor did any owls hoot. Utter silence, in that desolate night.

The building stood lone and isolated in the open plains atop the island where it looked out on the bleak never changing ocean. From the information she'd gathered from the locals back on land she learned that this medieval building was originally used as a monastery providing isolation from the outside world, its temptations and influences. Over numerous decades the archaic building had fallen into the operation of an order of the Magdalene sisters where it was used as a makeshift home for girls deemed unfit for their God fearing society. Prostitutes, the promiscuous, Mothers who were unwed, the retarded and the orphaned all knew this asylum where they would meet penance. What happened in between then and now that had caused the asylum to enter into this demonic state was a complete and utter mystery, one that no one in his or her right mind was willing to solve. It was unfortunate that the task of solving the mystery had fallen into her hands. She scanned the asylum over, sizing up how to penetrate its inhospitable outer. A grand and heavy wooden door was the obvious entrance through the jagged stone curtain around the monastery. All windows in her line of sight were covered with iron bars, which she wagered would support her bodyweight. These securities that once served to keep fallen girls in the asylum, now served to keep her out.

She felt her feet move from the springy unkempt grass to the uneven but firm worn stone pathway leading to the door of the asylum. The footsteps of her leathery boots sharpened from a grassy rustle to a distinct sharp clop as her soles met the gritty granite in a steady rhythm of steps. Armed with only a vague knowledge of the Hell she was about to encounter, she reflected back on the reading she had performed hours earlier on the main land. She'd spent her life as both a user and a slave to the occult. Its workings had become second nature to her. In a quiet corner of the tavern she rested in she'd shuffled the arcana almost unconsciously, their detailed illustrations folding and sliding into each other seamlessly in an order that the eye could not follow. Her mind focused on the vision she'd been presented with, the asylum and the need to know what it contained. The asylum she saw was no hazy image formed in the mind's eye, as a child seems images in the clouds. This was a vivid landscape branded into her mind by something not of this world, something that called out for her help as a medium and through these cards she could tell its story.

She placed the first card, 'The Moon', a warning of hidden dangers. All was not as it seemed and she would need to proceed carefully as danger lurked all around. 'The Ten of Swords', a card of ruin, telling the asylums long history of misery and despair and 'The Four of Swords', normally a symbol of recuperation as indicated by the withered rose it depicted, but this card was reversed, symbolizing the opposite; degradation and a poisoning of the internal mind.

Both 'The Devil' and 'The Tower' cards appeared side by side, a bizarre combination in almost any circumstance but this. 'The Devil' stood as a symbol of unbreakable bonds and prolonged suffering which seemed to almost contradict 'The Tower', a sudden change carried out with power to rival God's wrath or his intervention. The immovable object was about to collide with the unstoppable force.

'The King of Wands' card lay in between. A man intertwined in this dilemma, decisive and passionate but quick to anger as well as self-righteous, self-righteous to the point that bordered bigotry. His silhouette formed before her, deep in trance as she was. Who could this be? And quickly it was gone.

Finally 'The High Priestess' card concluded the reading. This card had one sure meaning; a secret was about to be revealed. She had the utmost confidence in the cards, and her own ability to read them. The accuracy of her predictions was notorious. She was held in high regard as both a talented medium and a cursed witch by the Romanys from whom she was descended.

Now looking clearly on the building there was no doubt she'd come to the right place. The image in her head matched perfectly with the landscape image before here, like a jigsaw piece neatly slotted together. Her strange mind was receptive to the malice pulsating from the building. It was unmistakable and it was nauseating.

She could wager to be inside it would be smothering at first. Her senses would be irritated and her thinking convoluted. Even a regular unreceptive mind would be heavily affected by its black, cursed aura. The place could possess its inhabitants with a deep depression that would fester in the mind. It would not be wise to stay within the building any longer than necessary.

She spied a protruding spire erect from the peak of the wall, conveniently above two horizontal stories of windows, both covered in jagged bars. After estimating it for a while, she began her ascent. Hoisting herself slowly above the bars, she gently lowered onto the blunt spikes slowly. Although painful the spikes were blunt enough she could support her full weight on them, at least long enough to stand and reach for the next level of bars in the above window and climb again. Repeating this method she managed to scale as high as the second floor. Unwisely looking down she became aware of how vital her balance was in this moment and she did her best to find it once more atop the spikes, despite her secret fear of heights. Now as high up as the windows would take her she removed the rope and the bar tied to it from her back. She lunged them upwards, hoping to catch them around the spire.

After several unsuccessful attempts the bar was caught in a narrow gap between the spire and a chimney parallel to it. Testing the rope was secure she threw caution to the wind and began to scale the bare wall of the building. With one last muster of strength she pulled herself above the ledge and awkwardly threw her leg over. With this she was able to shift her bodyweight to the other side and once again reclaimed some balance on the old cracked ceiling tiles. She had crossed the wall.

Placing her hand on the chimney top for support, she gathered herself and stood up straight to look upon the asylum. The silvery rooftops of the outer wall were outlined around her, extending from beneath her feet and stretching out beyond her view into the pale dimly lit mist that was descending upon the area rapidly. Below one of the far off spires with some effort she could discern the circular shape of a rose glass window above the entrance of what had been the monasteries chapel. She guessed she could see headstones at the base of the chapel but the mist had already claimed the ground, and her guess remained as just that, a guess.

She was at a loss to decide whether the sight of the gothic holy ground was beautiful or horrific.

Temporarily lost in the image, a crippling cold sensation seized her at the core. It was as if lightning made ice had struck her where she stood.

A man's silhouette, a distorted scream, blood.

All of these ran through her and in an instant were gone. Nearly losing her balance with fright she quickly regained her footing. Had that just happened? What exactly was it she just saw? She had embraced the sensation. She could feel the warmth of the blood on her hands, the sharp pang of the scream against her cold aching eardrums. And then just as suddenly it was gone. She was not amateur enough to lose herself to this. The asylum was swarmed with souls trapped in limbo. They were culminating, festering here. Like a person drowning, desperate to reach the air above, they would drag any medium, any link to the living world, down with them if given the chance.

Now after rallying, it was clear the gypsy's sense of sight was rendered useless in this mist. Unable to get a reliable picture of the monastery's layout, her attention turned to discovering a way into the asylum.

After a couple of moments scouting what little her limited visibility would allow, she secured the rope tightly around the chimney top in a simple, reliable six-knot and looping it between her hands began to slowly descend down the inner side of the wall. She was wise enough to know she could not depend on the aged, rickety roof tiles to support her. The windows on the inner side of the wall were thankfully unprotected by the bars that had served her so well on the outside and she was easily able to kick the fragile glass pane into shards that were swallowed in the dark she was about to enter. The rough gritty feeling of the rope began to ache against the skin of her hands like sand paper. She was constrained awkwardly with her weight on the rope rather than her feet, which were pressed against the vertical surface of the old bricks around the window.

Trying to manoeuvre herself through the pane, her side brushed against a remaining shard in the corner of the wooden panel where the glass pane had been shortly before. She felt her partially exposed thigh tear sharply beneath her skirt. The dirty, cloudy glass buried into it as she swung through the panel on the rope, opening a fine rift in the skin beneath her tights. For a moment she felt nothing, her cold frigid skin numbed by the cold of the night. Then a searing pain erupted through and through the gash bright, oxygenated blood now began to seep. Her eyes clenched tightly shut as she tried to block out the warm, pang of pain. The sound of crunching glass as her feet lowered and met the stone floor. Although she cursed violently under her breath, she was in at least and the relief of standing on her own two feet dulled the pain of the wound, if only slightly.

Regaining her composure, the gypsy surveyed her new surroundings. The vague silhouettes of furniture and ornaments were outlined dimly under the pale light hazing through where the window had been. Shards of shattered glass shimmered all over the floor. A distinct smell met her nostrils. She'd been exposed to the clear outside air for so long, and its absence was felt. The scent of oil stood out instantly, as well as the damp that accompanies any building of age, especially one so poorly kept as this.

She felt her way around the perimeter of the room awkwardly, her sense of touch being rekindled more with each different fibre now that she was no longer exposed to the numbing outside air. Eventually the oil lantern met her blind grasp.

She struck a match from a set she'd carried for safety and with the lantern lit, finally caught a glimpse of the room; once a type of lounge for what were the gatekeepers of the monastery.

Tall, stony, red-brick walls, shelves of tins, fractured pots cluttered together, a large fireplace in need of a good cleaning and a filthy copper kettle suspended above it on a stand. In the room's centre was a wooden table, fine and healthy looking, somewhat wasted in its grotty surroundings save for the conspicuous blood stains dried into it. It's a curious thing to ponder on how a spill of blood came to be. But she was denied time to ponder its history.

A distant noise met her ears from below. She crunched down as her hand made its way up her skirt. It's a well know truth that women contain more hiding places than men, a truth any streetwise woman makes full use of. Pressed between her inner thigh and the stretch band of her skirt was a knife. She clenched it tightly, ready to stab, should the need present itself.

The noise drew closer, became more distinct. It was a constant wailing noise. A cry, or was it a scream? She couldn't discern whether it belonged to a man or a woman but it was making its way up the steps. However no footsteps accompanied it. Perhaps it was another spectre, like the one that gripped her on the roof? No, this voice belonged to a body.   Along with the cries, which although unusual and distorted were sounding more and more infantile, she could now hear a limping noise accompanied by a dragging sound. It had rounded the top of the spiral staircase and was now crawling, dragging into the flickering light of the lantern.

She felt her throat gag violently, vomit in her stomach jolting as her eyes fixed on it.

The cause of screaming was now clear. These were screams of agony. The mass of limbs, haphazardly stitched together all covered in pulsing veins with no clear path for their blood to flow; the thick arms of men and women that clawed and dragged the creature along the ground, its fingernails shattered and torn off from digging against the stone floor.

Legs hung from it although largely unusable with no ability to grab or clutch and being stitched horizontally to the body, unable to stand. Protruding from an unidentifiable heap in the centre, an infant formed from the torso up. Serving as the eyes and ears, the damned child directed the actions of the abomination and led it up the stairs towards her. Its skin a corpse like grey, covered in blue and red veins and arteries, bulging where each ran.

The screaming sobs of pain gave her a horrific realisation; this creature was no roaming un-dead. Born from twisted alchemy, it was alive.

THE JOURNEYMAN

LEE MITCHELL

A tale I always like to tell
And one you'll know is true
Is the story of The Journeyman
Begot in 1832

A leap year full of choleric days
The year Dunelm took flight
Our hero, the aforementioned Journeyman
Was born one squalling night

Borne of hag and Royal stock
A stunning baby boy
Ebony hair and ivory skin
The mix of bold and coy

His Father, an ignoble Nobleman
With a beauty only skin-deep
Dashed the Mother's brains out
 Snatching Baby in his sleep

The Nobleman gave his son no name
Giving roof and a wet-nurse in lieu
The nurse bore her breast, to feed the babe
Babe bit the nurse, clean through!

Aghast, the nurse was screaming
'A portentous day is this!
'A Daemon you've brought to this house'
With that, the babe did hiss!

The hissing babe grew to a child,
And from child grew to a man,
Never named, just referred to as
The bastard Journeyman

His Father would not let him be
The heir to all his worth
Instead he made him work for all
His staff, labourers and serfs

Every day, he grafted hard
From morn' to eventide
Never given any help or praise
Taking each day in his stride

He used his time and solitude
To plan his future out
His plot to avenge his Mother's death
How he could make it come about

Near the end of his seventeenth year
He met his one true love
A striking miss of Irish blood
He thought sent from God above

Her equine skills exemplary
No stallion she couldn't tame
But mystery surrounded her
None knew her pride or shame

She spoke to our young Journeyman

And told him of her kin
Of Irish mystics and country folk
Songs of virtue, tales of sin

'My Mother told me every day',
The Irish miss proclaimed
'That the man who I was doomed to love
I'd have to give a name'

In turn our quiet journeyman
Spoke about his past
Of memories he shouldn't have
And dreams he had amassed

'I never knew the woman who,
Birthed me in to the world,
She haunts my thoughts each time I sleep'
The Irish miss was told

But on the very day he met her
His Father paid a call
And spotted the young Irish miss
Like his son, he was enthralled

The Nobleman offered the miss some work
To aid him at his feasts
She did not dare refuse the post
And left behind her beasts

All the days, the Irish miss
Cleaned for the master's pleasure
But through the night, she hid herself
And refused to be his treasure

One stormfilled night, he came to her
Dressed only in his drawers

He asserted his imperious power
And abused her on the floor

This crime became a nightly thing
The Irish Miss was his possession
She retreated to her inner world
Of numbness and suppression

The news of his true love's abuse
Was broken to our Journeyman
It added to his vitriol
And it was time to make a stand

Our hero sneaked away that day
To avenge the sick attacks
He found the miss upon her bed
And though day, the sky turned black

His former nursemaid, from her room
Saw him enter and decried him still
'He tasted blood, while in his crib
And now he brings ill will'

In the midday darkness, the young man and miss
Gazed deep into the others heart
His love for her was mirrored back
A bond that none could part

'My people have use of magics
And power beyond their measure
This night filled day is perfect for
Spells to rid us of our displeasure'

Unphased by her straightforwardness
The journeyman stood true
'It's said that I'm of daemon stock
And I will follow you'

'My love, it's time you had a name
One that's apt, and never wrong
Forget that bastard Journeyman
I name you Freeman Strong!'

Together they began to pray
Not to heaven nor to hell
Then at that time, the door flung wide
And the master's temper began to swell

'I pay for you to serve me alone
Step away from this bastard's side!
Get back to work you filthy scum
And I may just let this slide!'

The young miss and our protagonist
Hands clasped, they did not respond
As one, now and forever
Broken free of their master's bonds

The sight of them together
Brought gall to the master's throat
'I should have killed you with that slut
You ungrateful little scrote!'

An explosion then shook the mansion house
And as his words took form
A bolt of lightning reigned straight down
With no thunder, nor a storm

The master took the brunt of it
And fires began to burn
The miss and her Freeman Strong
Walked away without concern

Once outside, the day returned
Light shone from the sun above
Together now, no one can part
My parents free to love

NOTES ON CONTRIBUTORS

Foreword
William Hughes is Professor of Gothic Studies at Bath Spa University, Joint President of the International Gothic Association, founder editor of the internationally refereed journal "Gothic Studies", a prominent member of the editorial board of MUP's International Gothic Series and one of the two editors of the Edinburgh University Press Companions series.

His fifteen published books include *Beyond Dracula: Bram Stoker's Fiction and its Cultural Context* (2000), *Bram Stoker: A Bibliography* (1997), an annotated edition of Stoker's faux vampire novel *The Lady of the Shroud* (2001) and an annotated student edition of *Dracula* (2007), Reader's Guides to Dracula for Palgrave(2009) and Continuum (2009) and *The Historical Dictionary of Gothic Literature* (2013). Bill is the acknowledged leading World authority on Bram Stoker and star of the TV paranormal series Most Haunted.

Editor
Colin Younger is Programme Leader for English Literature and Creative Writing at the University of Sunderland. A published poet, song writer and scholar of Borders Theory, his works include *Border Crossings: Narration, Nation and Imagination in Scots and Irish Literature and Culture*, (2013) and forthcoming publications on Borders Gothic and the Folkloric Vampire (2014).

Mike Adamson has been an academic for many years, first as a student, then a tutor, at Flinders University of South Australia since 1993. Having recently had his Doctorate conferred Mike also holds Bachelor's Degrees in marine biology and archaeology, plus Honours and Masters Degrees in the latter, Mike has a wide range of skills and interests, and has presented academic papers at conferences locally and overseas.

Paul Alderson holds a first class BA (Hons) in English & Creative Writing from The University of Sunderland. He is currently an exciting new author of short stories.

Lindsay Bingham is a member of the South Shield's Writers Group and enjoys creative writing especially the short story.

Franklin Bishop is the author of John William Polidori: *'The Vampyre' and Other Writings* (2005), *Polidori! A Life of Dr. John Polidori* (1991), *Selected Works of John Polidori* (1991), and numerous articles on Gothic and Romantic literary figures. He is the acknowledged leading World authority on John Polidori and is also Keeper of

Newstead Abbey. A freelance journalist and writer, he is also a tutor for the University of Nottingham, Continuing Education Department.

Chloe Charlton holds a first class BA (Hons) in English & Creative Writing from The University of Sunderland.

David Craig is a graduate of St. Mary's College Twickenham. He is an accomplished musician, songwriter and has also written a number of short stories.

Kirstie Groom holds a first class BA (Hons) in English & Creative Writing from The University of Sunderland where she is currently a post-graduate student reading English Studies.

Elizabeth Hazlett holds a BA (Hons) in English & Creative Writing from The University of Sunderland where she is currently a post-graduate student reading English Studies.

Willy Maley is a critic, editor, teacher, and writer. A former Scotsman Fringe First Winner at the Edinburgh Festival (1992), his eight plays, mostly co-authored or collaborative include *From The Calton to Catalonia* (1990), a dramatized account of his father's experiences as a POW during the Spanish Civil War, co-written with his brother John Maley. In 1995, Willy founded with the late Philip Hobsbaum the Creative Writing postgraduate programme at Glasgow University. Since then, Willy has published on Renaissance literature from Shakespeare to Milton, and on modern Scottish and Irish writing, from De Valera to Devolution.

Michelle McCabe is an enthusiastic creative writer and is currently reading English & Creative Writing at The University of Sunderland.

Katie McMahon is an Academic at a North Eastern University. She is also a gifted creative writer.

Lee Mitchell recently graduated with a BA (Hons) in English & Creative Writing from The University of Sunderland.

Conor O'Donovan studied English & Creative Writing at the University of Sunderland for a short time on an exchange from The University of Ireland.

Nicola Rooks is a keen creative writer and is currently reading English & Creative Writing at The University of Sunderland.

Mary Ross is originally from South Tyneside where her imagination frequently got the better of her and she now lives in Southern Devon with her beloved husband and the ghosts of two cats.

Jamie Spears from Boston, USA holds Bachelor's and Master's degrees from The University of Sunderland and is currently a PhD student at the same institution.

John Strachan is Professor of English at Bath Spa University. He has previously taught at the universities of Northumbria, Oxford and Sunderland. His poetry has appeared in several magazines and collections.

Glenn Upsall is a screenwriter and author of short stories. He is Chair of the South Shields Writer's Group.

Steve Willis graduated in English at The University of Sunderland in 2012. He is also a talented creative writer.

Caitlin Wilson holds a BA (Hons) in English & Creative Writing from The University of Sunderland where she is currently a post-graduate student reading English Studies.

Alison Younger is Programme Leader for MA English Studies at the University of Sunderland. An extremely talented critical and creative writer, her publications include: *Representing Ireland: Past, Present and Future*, (2005), *Essays on Modern Irish Literature*, (2007), *Ireland at War and Peace* (2011), *No Country for Old Men: Fresh Perspectives on Irish Literature,* (2008) and *Celtic Connections: Irish-Scottish Relations and the Politics of Culture* (2012).

Printed in Great Britain
by Amazon.co.uk, Ltd.,
Marston Gate.